KT-467-791

Gunrage at Calder Wells

Marshal Jim Calladine had been hunting the outlaw Cal Forden, wanted for armed robbery, land thieving and gun-running to the Indians. Then murder was added to those crimes – with Calladine as the victim.

His brother, Steve, set out on a mission of vengeance. Following Jim's trail, Steve joined a wagon train heading west, passing near to Calder Wells where Forden held sway. Steve might never have reached the town had it not been for Melanie Ridgeway, who saved his life when their wagon train came under Indian attack.

But this was only the start of his problems, and if Steve was to survive to face Forden he was going to need all the help he could get.

COUNTY LIBRARY

Cork City Library
WITHDRAWN
FROM STOCK

Gunrage at Calder Wells

Robert J. Evers

A Black Horse Western

ROBERT HALE · LONDON

© John Glasby 2006
First published in Great Britain 2006

ISBN-10: 0-7090-7984-2
ISBN-13: 978-0-7090-7984-2

Robert Hale Limited
Clerkenwell House
Clerkenwell Green
London EC1R 0HT

The right of John Glasby to be identified as
author of this work has been asserted by him
in accordance with the Copyright, Designs and
Patents Act 1988.

CORK CITY
LIBRARY
529|587

BISHOPSTOWN
LIBRARY

Typeset by
Derek Doyle & Associates, Shaw Heath.
Printed and bound in Great Britain by
Antony Rowe Limited, Wiltshire.

CHAPTER I

TRAIL TOWN

The continuous rain had turned the streets of Clinton into a morass of brown mud. Outside the stores, the awnings constantly dripped water onto the already sodden boardwalks. Overhead, ominous dark clouds, sweeping in from the distant mountains, gave dire warning that the rain would continue unabated for some considerable time.

Axle-deep in the tenacious mud, the long line of covered wagons stood along the main street. There were nineteen in all, making this one of the largest trains to leave Clinton for more than three years. Others had set out in the past, some from Clinton and more from the various frontier towns.

How many of them had got through to where the trails west ended at the California border, no one knew. Many had perished on the way at the hands of warlike Indian tribes, outlaws and even natural catastrophes. Yet still they kept coming, hardy men and staunch, determined women, heading for the promised land and a better life.

Slipping and sliding helplessly, the men cursed as they struggled to get the horses and oxen between the shafts. Women and children, drenched to the skin, moved in and out of the various stores, carrying large sacks of provisions.

Standing just inside the doorway of his office, out of the teeming rain, Sheriff Sam Dexter ran a critical eye over the train. Over the past fifteen years he had seen these wagons come and go, heading for California. Inwardly, he wondered how many of them had succeeded in getting through.

Not many, he figured. Most of them would undoubtedly have been attacked by marauding Indians or were lost somewhere in the alkali flats fifty miles west of Clinton. Yet still they came, searching for gold, or just a better life than they'd had back east.

He chewed reflectively on the wad of tobacco, then glanced round swiftly at the sound of an approaching rider. He narrowed his eyes a little. The man who sat the large black stallion was also dressed in black.

Dexter's keen gaze took in the twin Colts and the Winchester in the scabbard and felt a little warning tingle run along his spine. Immediately he had the other figured for a gunhawk or a lawman but there was no star on the man's shirt.

Sliding easily from the saddle, the rider looped his mount's reins over the rail and stepped up onto the boardwalk.

'Guess you're the sheriff here,' he said. 'Maybe you can help me.'

'Depends,' Dexter muttered shortly. 'You lookin' for somebody?'

The other gave a brief nod. Taking off his hat, he dashed the rain from the brim. 'Can we talk inside? This ain't the sort o' weather to stand out here.'

Dexter hesitated. There was something about this man that worried him. The other didn't look like the ordinary run of killers he'd come up against in the past but he felt certain the man facing him knew how to use the guns at his waist.

Spitting the wad of tobacco into the street, he stood on one side and motioned the other inside. Seating himself in the chair behind the desk, he motioned towards the other.

'Mind tellin' me your name, mister?' he said finally. 'I kinda like knowin' who I'm talkin' to.'

'The name's Calladine, Steve Calladine. I'm here lookin' for my brother.'

'Calladine.' Dexter scratched his chin. It made a scratching sound, just audible against the rain hammering at the window. 'The name's familiar, but I don't—'

'He's a Federal marshal. Last I heard from him, he was headed this way hopin' to get the lowdown on someone named Cal Forden.'

A gust of expression flashed over the sheriff's features. 'Now I remember. He did ride into Clinton, three or four months back He didn't wear a star, said he was workin' undercover.'

'You know what happened to him?'

7

'Not much. I told him I couldn't help him. There's no one by the name o' Forden in Clinton. All I know is he took the trail west.'

Steve glanced up, his eyes narrowed. 'What's out there? Any more towns like this where he might be?'

'Not towns like this, mister.' There was a note of sardonic amusement in the lawman's voice. 'Once you get across the border, twenty miles from here, you're in outlaw and Indian country. There are a couple o' towns along the trail west of here but they ain't the sort o' places I'd advise anyone to visit.'

'Why not?'

Dexter uttered a short laugh. 'Guess you don't know much of this country, Mister Calladine. We got some kind o' law and order here in Clinton. Forty miles or so west of here, you'll reach Yellow Buttes and then there's Calder Wells. There it's the law of the gun. Start askin' any awkward questions and you'll catch a bullet quicker than you can blink.'

He rolled himself a cigarette, thrust it between his lips and lit it. 'They're both helltowns. Any wagon trails leavin' here for the west steer well clear of 'em. Even then I've heard of some trains that never got to wherever they were goin'. If your brother went to Yellow Buttes or Calder Wells as an undercover Federal marshal, I'd say he'll be damned lucky if he's still alive.'

Calladine gave a terse nod. 'You know, Sheriff, that's just what I've been thinkin'.' There was a hard set to his jaw that the other noticed at once.

'Guess I know how you're feeling but if I were you, I'd steer clear of those places. You'll only be headin' into big trouble if you don't.'

Steve pushed back the chair and got to his feet. 'Thanks for the advice, Sheriff.' Moving to the door, he paused and glanced back. 'That wagon train out there. You got any idea if they'll be passing close to—?'

Dexter interrupted him sharply. 'Pretty close, I reckon, but I know Hap Disforth, the wagon-master, and he don't like solitary strangers travelling with him, particularly anyone who has the look of a gunfighter about him.'

'Guess I'll have a word with him anyway,' Steve said. Thrusting open the door, he stepped outside into the rain.

While the stores were being loaded into the wagons, Hap Disforth rode slowly along the train, checking that everything was going smoothly and it would be possible to move out before dark. He was a tall man, his piercing grey eyes above the sharp nose and black moustache taking in every little detail. It was his responsibility to ensure that nothing was left; that as far as possible, everyone knew what lay ahead of them.

He had no illusions about the journey that faced them. Once they left Clinton, the land they entered was sparsely populated, a lawless country where for everybody it was a question of struggling to survive against a hard, bitter nature that wanted nothing of men.

Added to this, there were bands of marauding Indians and outlaws with the habits of prairie wolves, men who preyed on the wagon trains driving west.

He reined his mount at the front of the train. Here, the four horses were already in the traces, pawing the sticky ground nervously as if anxious to be away.

'You got everything on board, Herb?' he asked.

'Reckon so.' Herb Wisley gave a nod of affirmation. He pulled his leather jerkin more tightly about his shoulders. 'Hell, but I'll be glad to get out o' this goddamn rain.'

He threw a quick glance into the rear of the wagon where a woman and two small children were seated. Grimly, he said, 'Anywhere would be better than this.'

Hap shook his head. 'Once we hit the Badlands, you'll all be prayin' for rain.'

'That bad?'

'Reckon you'll find out once we get there. Those flats are nothin' but white alkali for scores o' miles under a sun hotter than the hinges o' hell.'

'You done this before?' Wisley queried.

'Twice, and believe me, it ain't easy,' muttered the other. 'It's well over a thousand miles from here to the California border and there's danger every mile o' the way. I just hope you and the others back there know what's in front of you.'

'We know it ain't goin' to be easy,' Wisley replied. 'But there's nothin' here for us. Martha and me talked it over for some time before we decided to head out west with the kids.'

'Guess everyone has a dream.' Hap made to say something more, then turned his head quickly at the sound of the approaching rider.

He eyed the man apprehensively, noting the Colts

10

carried low at the waist in well-oiled holsters. His first impression was the same as the sheriff's – this man was either a gunfighter or a lawman.

The other reined up a couple of feet away. 'You Disforth, the wagon-master?' Calladine asked, his voice deceptively quiet.

Disforth gave a stiff nod. 'That's right, mister. I'm takin' this train all the way to California.'

'You got room for one more?'

Hap narrowed his eyes, suspicion on his bluff features. 'I don't take on loners,' he replied sharply. 'Especially men I know nothin' about. You on the run from the law?'

'If I was on the run from the law, I'd ride straight on and keep goin'. But I've got business in Yellow Buttes and Calder Wells.'

Disforth's suspicion mounted rapidly. 'Calder Wells! That's some seventy miles west from here. A frontier helltown if there ever was one.'

Herb leaned sideways a little, running the reins through his fingers. 'Just who are you, mister?' he asked thinly. 'Reckon if we were to take you along with us, we should know somethin' about you.'

'The name's Steve Calladine. I don't know much about this country but I've heard there are Cherokee and Apache in these parts and I figure you could use an extra gun if you're hopin' to cross it.'

'I'm well aware of what lies out there,' Disforth snapped. 'But you seem like a man used to ridin' a lonely trail. Why would you want to take up with us?'

Steve shrugged. 'Sometimes a man likes company along the trail,' he said thinly. 'But suit yourself.'

Wheeling his mount, he made to ride away then stopped as the wagon-master called out, 'All right, Calladine. It's against my better judgement but I guess you can ride with the train. From what I see of you, I reckon you know how to use those guns.'

'When I have to. When do you move out?'

'Just as soon as the animals are hitched and the stores loaded on board.'

Touching his hand to his hat, Steve nodded and rode back towards the end of the train, head lowered against the slashing rain.

Hap watched him go, then turned to face Wisley. 'Can't say I like the look of him,' he remarked. 'He's got the look of a killer about him.'

'Ain't there been some talk o' gold being found out west? Could be that's what he's a-lookin' for.'

Disforth shook his head emphatically. 'He's no prospector. If it's gold he wants, it's more likely he'll rob some bank or stage. I figure it would be wise to keep an eye on him while he's ridin' with us.'

An hour later, with the horses and oxen straining against the clinging mud, the train moved out of Clinton. In a loose line they set out across the grassland, the wagons swaying precariously as they hit the rocky, uneven trail.

At the rear, Steve rode in silence, knowing that most of the folk in the train were already suspicious of the stranger riding with them, wondering who he was, why he was there.

Circling the wagons, Disforth dropped back until he was riding alongside him.

'All right, Calladine,' he said tautly. 'Now suppose

you tell me what's so important about gettin' to Yellow Buttes and Calder Wells.' There were taut lines etched across the wagon-master's face. 'Tell me if I'm wrong, but my guess is that you're out for revenge. Nobody who's right in the head would ride all of the way to those helltowns for nothin'.'

Steve pressed his lips tightly together, then said harshly, 'Last I heard from my brother, he was headin' this way on the trail of some *hombre* named Forden. That was some three months ago. I've heard nothin' since.'

'You think he's been killed?'

'I don't think. From what I've heard, I'm damned sure he has. If that's the case, I intend to find out who killed him and hunt the critter down if it's the last thing I do.'

'From what I know o' those places, it probably will be the last thing you do,' Hap retorted grimly. 'Those towns are a nest o' snakes of the worst kind; crooked gamblers, rustlers, gunhawks, killers on the run. You name it and you'll find it there. There ain't no law and order, probably never will be.'

'You know anythin' of those towns?' Steve asked, suddenly interested.

'Been to Calder Wells once and that was one time too many. Lucky to get out with a whole skin.'

He eyed Steve speculatively for a long moment, then went on, 'Guess it's none o' my business but if your brother's dead, nothin' you can do will bring him back. You won't have a chance o' finding his killer. Nobody will talk. Best thing you can do is stick with the train and head on west with us.'

'Afraid that's somethin' I can't do,' Steve said, his clenched teeth showing whitely in the faint light.

'No, I guess not.' The other waited for a moment and then, when Steve remained silent, he dug his spurs into his mount's flanks and rode quickly along the snaking column.

They made camp where a long stand of trees bordered the trail. The rain had eased a little but with the coming of night a wind had got up, gusting from the south. Steve sat with his back against a tall tree, a short distance from the camp.

Fires had been lit and several of the women were preparing a meal. Nearby, the stallion grazed on the tall grass. There was some dried beef in his saddlebag and water in his canteen.

Getting to his feet, he moved towards his mount, then stopped abruptly at a soft sound behind him. Turning, he saw the girl standing hesitantly a few feet away. Tall and slim, he could just make out her features in the dimness, the long chestnut hair flowing over her shoulders. She held something in her hands.

'I thought you might be hungry,' she said in a low, husky voice. 'I've brought you some stew.'

'Thanks. That's mighty kind of you, Miss—'

'Ridgeway, Melanie Ridgeway.' She eyed him with a frank, steady gaze as he seated himself on the grass, spooning the stew into his mouth. 'You joined the wagon train back there in Clinton, didn't you? We'd all been gathering there for more than three weeks and I'd never seen you before.'

'That's right.'

'Are you travelling all the way to California with us?'

He shook his head. 'I'm just ridin' with the train as far as Yellow Buttes.' After a brief pause he added, 'If I don't find what I'm lookin' for there, I might catch up with you somewhere along the trail and then head for Calder Wells.'

Melanie gave him a shrewd glance. 'You must be looking for something really important to go to all that trouble.'

'Guess I am.' After a short silence he asked, 'Are you travellin' alone?'

'No. My father's back there near the wagon. My mother died two years ago and he couldn't stay. Too many memories, I guess.'

'If you make it, I reckon you'll find California a little different from back east. It's a whole new country.'

'They say there are plenty of opportunities for anyone wanting to settle there.'

'Sure. But there'll be plenty o' folk hopin' to get rich quick and some of 'em won't mind how they do it.'

Handing the empty bowl back to her, he nodded his thanks. After a moment, she left and he watched her dim shape walking back to one of the nearer wagons.

Rolling himself into his blankets, he lay on his back staring up at the sky. They were still close enough to Clinton to be relatively safe from any danger. But that would not last for long. While in town, he had asked a few questions waiting for the wagon train to move out.

From what he had learned, it seemed that a number of attacks had been made on the town. Bands of Indians had hit the outskirts in the not too distant past. Now, he wondered if the wagon-master, or any of the others, had discovered this disturbing fact for themselves. Somehow he doubted it, but soon they would be heading into Indian territory and that was where the trouble would start.

Mid-morning, two days later, found the train labouring across rugged, treacherous terrain. The rain had stopped the previous afternoon and the sky was clear and blue all the way to the horizon. Half an hour earlier they had entered a long decline and now the animals were finding it difficult to haul the heavy wagons along the rocky trail.

Tall bluffs rose on one side and, in places, the men were forced to get down and help pull the wheels free of deep ruts. Riding forward, Steve found Disforth near the front of the column. The wagon-master had dismounted and, with the driver, was straining to dislodge one of the wheels where it had caught against a large boulder.

Disforth glanced up sharply as Steve said, 'Guess I'll ride on ahead and scout out the territory.'

Disforth nodded his acquiescence but said nothing.

Touching spurs to the stallion's flanks, Steve put the horse into a brisk gallop. The high bluff extended for a further mile and then ended sharply as if cut off by a knife. The sparse grass also stopped

16

at almost the same place.

Up ahead was rough, open country where it was almost impossible to make out any trail. The sun was now climbing towards its zenith and it beat down in scorching waves on his back and shoulders.

Sitting easily in the saddle, he built a smoke, inhaling deeply as he scanned the terrain all around him, his keen gaze searching for any sign of movement. Away to his left, perhaps three miles distant, was a large escarpment thrusting out of the mesa like a hog's back. Further to the west were other ridges, black with shadow.

Carefully, he swept his gaze over them, then stiffened. Narrowing his eyes against the sunglare, he made out the smoke. It showed just above the centre of the escarpment, white against the washed-out blue of the sky and, swinging his gaze westward, he picked out a second signal some distance ahead.

Pulling hard on the reins, he wheeled his mount and rode back. By the time he reached the train it had edged out of the rocky defile into the open. Disforth was riding a short distance in front.

'There's trouble ahead,' Steve called.

'What sort o' trouble?' Hap asked tersely.

'Indians. I've just seen their smoke. Reckon they know you're here.' He pointed to a spot almost half a mile ahead. 'Better get everyone ready and out yonder.'

Without asking any questions, Hap rode back along the column, urging them forward. Not until the last wagon was well clear of the rocks did they halt.

17

'You got any idea how many Indians there are?' Disforth queried. He turned his head slowly to take in all of the seeable view. 'I don't see any smoke now.'

'It was there all right. No mistakin' it. I'm fairly sure they've split their force into two groups. If there are enough of 'em they'll attack soon. If not, they may wait until we're closer to those hills yonder and hit us from two sides.'

Hap ran a finger down the side of his nose. 'I'd say they'll prefer the latter. Those rocks yonder will give 'em plenty of cover. I say we stay here where we can see 'em coming for miles.'

'Then set the wagons in a big circle yonder. If they do mean to attack, it's best we force 'em to do it on ground of our choosin', not theirs.'

Fortunately, before setting out from Clinton, all of the drivers had been primed on what to do in the event of an attack, whether from Indians or outlaws. Five minutes later, they were all in position with everyone inside the circle of cover provided by the wagons.

With the women and children inside, under canvas, the men waited around the perimeter, rifles and revolvers ready in their hands. Eyeing them critically, Steve wondered how many of them were adept in the use of these weapons. Not many, he reflected.

He glanced up at the man a few feet away. Like himself, the other was dressed in black and from his collar, Steve guessed he was a preacher. Feeling Steve's gaze on him, the other turned. 'You really think these Indians will attack us?' he asked uncertainly.

18

'It's hard to say, Reverend,' Steve replied. 'But out here you have to be prepared for anythin'.'

'But it isn't as if we're going to take any of their land,' the other protested. 'All we want to do is cross it and then leave them in peace.'

'Evidently you know nothin' of these critters. There are two things they want from these wagons, rifles and whiskey. Sometimes you can buy 'em off by giving them whiskey but that's a double-edged sword. They might just leave you alone if you hand it to 'em. But then, once they get themselves drunk on that firewater, they'll just as readily slaughter everyone on the train. The only thing that will save our skins is this.'

He held up the Winchester he had taken from his saddle. 'Do you have a gun, Reverend?'

'I'm afraid that in my line of work, I find such weapons unnecessary.'

'Then I guess you'd better get back inside that wagon and lie flat on the floor because these savages don't believe in your God.' He glanced swiftly to his right. 'And it looks as though we're in for a fight.'

Along the rugged top of the escarpment, a long line of dark figures was just visible. From what he could see, he reckoned there were about a score of them. A moment later, the Indians put their ponies to the steep downgrade, descending in an obscuring cloud of dust, which temporarily hid them from view.

Glancing round to his right, he saw that he had not been mistaken in his earlier surmise. A second group was riding swiftly from the west, converging on the train.

19

'Everybody get down!' Disforth's hard, authoritative voice shouted the order from the far side of the circle. 'And make every shot count. If we can take out most of 'em, there's a chance the rest will scatter.'

A shot rang out from somewhere close by. It was answered by Disforth's harsh yell. 'Hold your fire, damn you, until they get closer. There ain't any sense in wastin' ammunition.'

As they came closer, Steve recognized the enemy as Cherokee. As far as their total numbers were concerned, it was difficult to make any accurate estimate but he guessed there were at least fifty altogether.

His gaze roved restlessly ahead of him, his finger bar straight on the trigger. As if at a given signal, the Cherokee divided into two groups while they were still some three hundred yards away. One bunch swept off to the left, whooping loudly. The other plunged straight for the train.

Gently, he squeezed the trigger. The Winchester slammed against his shoulder. With a sense of satisfaction, he saw one of the braves throw up his arms and pitch from the saddle. Swiftly, he aimed again and a second went down. Around the perimeter of the circle, the rest of the men were firing into the milling enemy.

A shower of arrows arced downward. Several embedded themselves in the canvas of the wagons and a short distance away, one of the defenders fell back with a loud cry of agony, clutching his right shoulder where an arrow had penetrated.

More of the attacking Cherokee tumbled into the

dust as a second volley of gunfire tore into them. The others had now completely encircled the wagon train, racing their ponies in a wide ring.

Two fire arrows passed over Steve's head. One struck the ground a couple of feet behind his outstretched legs, extinguishing itself immediately. The second, however, hit the canvas cover of the nearby wagon. Flames took hold instantly but within seconds, two of the women clambered down, hauling two water buckets from the side and throwing the contents onto the fire.

Not taking time to reload the rifle, Steve pulled the Colts from their holsters. Even as he did so, one of the attackers suddenly swerved his mount, coming straight for him. Instinctively, he rolled over onto his side as the palomino leapt over the shafts and landed within inches of his legs.

The brave slid off his mount and was on his feet a moment later. The tomahawk in his hand came swinging down towards Steve's head. There was no time to move away.

Desperately, he tried to bring up his guns, knowing there was no chance of hitting the other before the brightly gleaming blade descended.

Then, without warning, the Cherokee lurched sideways. His back arched as the tomahawk fell from his nerveless fingers, thudding into the ground close to Steve's arm. The Indian's eyes went wide with shock as he swayed for a few moments before crashing against the wagon wheel. A trickle of blood oozed from the corner of his slackly open mouth.

Steve's first impression was that the preacher had,

21

somehow, overcome his natural repugnance for killing. Then he saw Melanie Ridgeway standing a few feet away holding a smoking Colt in her hand. She lowered the weapon slowly, shaking slightly, and there was an expression in her eyes Steve couldn't analyse.

'Thanks,' he said hoarsely. 'I guess you saved my life. Now get down. They ain't finished with us yet.'

Hesitating for only an instant, she went down onto her knees beside him, crouching down as more arrows thudded among the wagons.

'I shot him, didn't I?' There was a slight tremor in her voice. 'I killed him.'

'It's lucky for me that you did. Another second and it would've been me lying there. I know how you feel but he won't be the last before you reach the end o' this trail.'

Five minutes later, the band of Cherokee withdrew, halting their mounts out of gunshot range. Around the circle of wagons at least a score of bodies lay strewn on the rocks.

'Why have they stopped?' Melanie asked tautly.

Thrusting more shells into the Winchester, Steve said grimly, 'They're countin' their losses. That first attack was just to test our defences. Now they know we can give a good account of ourselves, they may decide to withdraw.'

'Do you think they'll attack again?'

'It's possible, I reckon. Depends on their chief and how much they want what we've got in the wagons. They may decide to wait until dark and then try a sneak attack. They know we can't stay here forever.'

Disforth came walking over. 'We've beaten them off for the time bein',' he grated. 'Could be they'll think twice before attackin' us again.'

'What about our casualties?' Steve asked.

'Guess we were fortunate. Two men wounded but I figure they'll live.'

He threw a hard glance at the girl. 'What the hell are you doin' here?' he demanded roughly. 'I gave orders that all the women were to stay inside the wagons. Do you want to get yourself killed?'

Before Melanie could make any reply, Steve butted in. 'Hold hard there, Hap. I wouldn't be alive if it hadn't been for her.' He jerked a thumb towards the dead Cherokee.

'It was still a damnfool thing to do,' said the other grudgingly. 'This ain't women's work.'

Jerking up his head from his scrutiny of the dead brave, he said, 'It looks as though they've had enough. They're pullin' out.'

Lifting himself cautiously, Steve peered into the sun-hazed distance. It seemed that what the other said was true. The Cherokee had turned their ponies and were heading back in the direction of the escarpment. Breathing a sigh of relief, he stood up and held out his hand to help Melanie to her feet.

With the moon almost full and a clear, starlit night, there was sufficient light for Steve to make out details all around the camp. Disforth had decided they should remain where they were throughout the day and settle there for the night.

There had been no further sign of the Cherokee

during the remainder of the day. With the heat lying over the plain like the inside of an oven they had remained alert, lying in any shade they could find. Now, with the coming of darkness, a coolness spread over the plain.

Disforth seemed to have lost most of his earlier suspicion of Steve and, an hour before, they had settled on setting a watch throughout the night. Four of them were in position to keep constant watch in every direction. Now Steve sat with his shoulders against one of the wheels and listened to the deep, eternal silence of the night.

For a moment, the image of Melanie Ridgeway standing there with the Colt in her hand, popped into his mind. Then he drew himself together and pushed it savagely into the background of his thoughts. That was something he didn't dare to think about.

Other matters crowded to the forefront of his mind, blotting out everything else. Sometime, somewhere, he would come face to face with the man he was now sure had killed his brother. Whether in Yellow Buttes or Calder Wells or some other frontier town along the border, that moment would come. Only then, when that man lay dead at his feet, would he be free of this all-consuming desire for vengeance, which had been riding him every moment of the day and night.

One of the horses snickered. It was a soft sound in the distance but it brought him instantly alert, pulling his thoughts back to the present. Very slowly, he drew himself upright. Somewhere in the distance, new sounds lifted to disturb the clinging stillness. For a moment, he thought they were just the noises of nocturnal animals. Then tension gripped him as he realized they were more probably the Cherokee signalling among themselves, calling to each other.

As silently as a cat, he lowered himself onto his stomach and eased himself beneath the wagon. Straining his vision, he pushed his sight into the moonlit dimness, trying to make out any movement among the long shadows.

For a full five minutes, he saw nothing. Everything was quiet, too quiet. Then, slightly to his left, a shadow glided smoothly into a narrow defile. A moment later, a second slid behind a large boulder.

Easing the Winchester forward, he sighted on the boulder, waiting tensely, his finger hard on the trigger. Several seconds went by with an agonizing slowness. Then the Cherokee brave suddenly launched himself into the open, heading for the wagons.

Squeezing the trigger, he saw the other abruptly twist in midair, jerk as if he had slammed into an invisible wall. The heavy slug hurled him sideways. Simultaneously, other shots rang out, shattering the silence into screaming fragments.

As if his shot had been a signal, more of the Cherokee rose from the rocks, running forward, seemingly oblivious of the lead pouring into them. A dark shape suddenly materialized in front of Steve, leaping out of the darkness. The moonlight glinted briefly on the drawn knife in the other's right hand.

Wheeling sharply, somehow heaving himself to his feet, Steve threw himself at the other, the Winchester hard across the Cherokee's throat. Thrusting down, ignoring the brave's struggles, he increased the pressure. His adversary's eyes bulged from their sockets. A rasping whistle emerged from his throat as he tried to draw air into his heaving lungs. Slowly, his struggles became more feeble until, with a throaty rattle, his entire body went limp.

Straightening with an effort, Steve saw that the battle was almost over. The gunshots had roused everyone in the camp and by the time their combined fire ceased, more than a dozen dead Indians lay sprawled on the rocks. Barely half a dozen managed to melt away into the night.

CHAPTER II

NIGHT ATTACK

Two days later, the train was struggling across an arid land where the only things that moved were sand scorpions and the rolling tumbleweeds. Disforth had hoped to sight the river by the previous evening but either he had mistaken his bearings or the fight with the Cherokee had thrown them further off their planned route than he had anticipated.

Now he rode restlessly a little way ahead of the leading wagons, sitting slouched in the saddle, his hat-brim pulled well down over his eyes. Lines of worry furrowed his forehead. He barely turned his head as Steve drew level with him.

Through his teeth, he said hoarsely, 'We should have reached the river hours ago. Yet there ain't any sign of it.'

Nodding, Steve said, 'If it was anywhere close by, I reckon the horses would've scented water.'

'That's what I was thinkin'.' Taking his kerchief from around his neck, the other mopped his face.

27

Steve eyed him with a searching glance. 'You got somethin' else on your mind apart from reachin' water. What is it? You reckon those Indians might still try to attack?'

'Could be,' the wagon-master muttered. Lifting himself higher in the saddle, he pointed straight ahead. 'But it's a different kind o' danger I'm worried about. I've taken these trains out twice. That land on the other side o' the river might look empty, but it ain't. It's cattle country and the rancher who claims he owns it doesn't like folk crossin' his land.'

Steve rubbed a hand down the side of his face where the irritating grains of alkali had worked their way into the folds of flesh. 'Far as I know, this is open country, government land.'

'Sure it is, but with the nearest army post more than sixty miles away at Fort Augusta, the cattle barons are the law here and they enforce it with their hired gunmen. We had a run in with them the last time out and only just managed to fight 'em off.'

'And you reckon they'll do the same this time.'

'Damned sure they will. The last time we had half a dozen armed outriders with us. This time there are only you and the men in the wagons.'

'It is possible to skirt around them?'

'That would mean adding a hell of a time to the journey and that country is even worse than this. No, we have to push on until we're clear of the Cimarron. We've no other choice.'

Steve shrugged negligently. Changing the subject, he said tersely, 'I'll ride on ahead for a way, see if I can find the river. Even though there's been no sign of those Cherokee for a couple o' days, I have the feelin' we ain't seen the last o' them.'

Jerking on the reins, he put the stallion to a brisk gallop, leaving Disforth staring after him.

Out here, in the vast, open wilderness, there was no sign of any trail. Barren and blindingly white in the harsh sunlight, the flats formed a huge basin, ringed by high rock walls. Turning recent events over in his mind, he tried to estimate where the river lay. It would almost certainly be swollen by the rains of the previous week and the problem of getting the heavy wagons across if it was in full flood was one he didn't want to think about.

That, however, might be the least of their trouble. If the Cherokee were still determined to wipe them out and take whatever was in those wagons, they would know the train had to reach the river to replenish their dwindling supply of water and that was where they would almost certainly make their attack.

An hour later, he was nearing the high rocks that bordered the far edge of the flats. As far as he could determine, these extended in an unbroken line around the alkali. Reining up, he sat forward and built himself a smoke. The mountains lay far to the north, a saw-toothed ridge along the horizon, some white-topped with snow.

It would be there, he thought, that the river would have its beginning. From what Disforth had intimated, it then flowed south, running along the western rim of the flats. But from what he could see, there was no way out in this direction. It would be

29

impossible to take the wagons over these rocks, which effectively blocked any way off the plain.

Flicking the cigarette-butt away, he urged the stallion forward, his keen gaze scanning the terrain. Then, half a mile ahead, he spotted a dark shadow that had previously been hidden by a wide tongue of rock protruding into the alkali. Swiftly, he headed toward it.

Now he noticed how his mount pricked up its ears and needed no urging. The stallion smelled water and knew, by that strange instinct possessed by animals, where it was. The wide patch of darkness was an opening in the rock wall, earlier obscured by a curve in the rock.

Swinging his mount in a curve, he estimated that the aperture was wide enough to allow a couple of the big wagons through at a time, and as he emerged on the other side, he made out the river. It flowed less than half a mile away, turning in an acute angle on the far side of the rocky barrier.

Ten minutes later, he dropped lightly from the saddle and flung himself down on the bank, dousing his head in the icily cold water. A few feet away, the stallion drank noisily. Shaking the water from his hair, he got to his feet and surveyed the wide stretch of water. It looked deep near the middle and there the current was flowing swiftly. Crossing at this point would not be without its dangers, yet a glance up and downriver told him it was the best spot.

Speckles of white a mile or so to his left gave away the presence of rapids while in the other direction, more high rocks edged both banks. It was obvious that this was not the place where Disforth had intended crossing. From what he could judge, the trail they should have followed lay quite a distance further north.

Moving towards his mount, he stopped abruptly as a harsh voice said, 'Hold it right there, mister.'

Two men rode out from the shelter of the rocks a short distance away. Each man wore his guns low and there was a look of suspicion in their eyes as they came forward slowly.

One was tall and thin, his hard lips drawn back slightly across his teeth. The other was short and broad, clearly a Mexican half-breed, the sombrero tilted back on his head, looped around his chin on a black cord.

'You ain't figgerin' on crossing the river, are you?' asked the taller man silkily. 'That land over there belongs to Ed Casson and he don't like strangers on his range.'

'Ed Casson?' Steve put a note of enquiry into the words. 'Can't say I've heard of him. Far as I was aware, this is open government land.'

The Mexican showed his tobacco-stained teeth in a broad grin. 'There's no government out here, *amigo*. This land all the way to Yellow Buttes is Mister Casson's. He owns it all.'

Steve's tone was dangerously deceptive as he said, 'And if I was to figure on ridin' across it, what then?'

For a moment, a look of consternation flashed over the tall man's features. Then he narrowed his eyes down to mere slits and shifted slightly in the saddle. 'That would be very foolish. You'd be a dead man before you crossed half of it.'

He made to say something more but at that moment, the Mexican laid a hand on his arm. 'Perhaps this *hombre* is riding with that wagon train we saw a few miles back. Maybe he's ridden ahead to check things out.'

For a moment, a grim smile showed on the tall man's face. Then it was gone so quickly it was hard for Steve to be sure he had seen it. Jerking up his head, he said thinly, 'If you are, stranger, I suggest you ride back and tell those land-grabbers they'll be shot to pieces if they set foot on the other side of the river.'

Ignoring the fact that both men had their hands close to their Colts, Steve reached for the pommel and pulled himself smoothly into the saddle. Barely was he upright, than the Wincester was in his left hand, the barrel pointed directly at the two riders.

He saw the Mexican make a quick move towards his gun but his hand froze a couple of inches from it as Steve said coldly, 'Don't try it or I'll kill you both. You've given your warning. Now both of you put your mounts into the river and tell your boss we're drivin' straight across any land in our path. This train is headed for California and nothin' is going to stop us.'

Both men stared in silence at the speed with which the rifle had appeared in Steve's hand. Steve had recognized their kind at once. Gunslingers whose faces were on wanted posters in half a dozen states, men who were protected from the law only so long as they carried out the dirty work for the big cattlemen who hired them.

'If you and your friends back there trespass on Casson's land, you'll all regret it,' the tall gunhawk hissed, his tone full of menace. 'He's got fifty men on his payroll and I don't reckon those men with that wagon train will stand a chance against them.'

With a sharp gesture to his companion, he pulled savagely on the reins and put the horse into the water. After a brief pause, the Mexican followed.

Turning in the saddle, the tall man glared at Steve. 'You'll regret this, my friend,' he grated harshly. 'One day you and I are going to meet again and then you won't have the drop on me. When that day comes, I'm going to kill you.'

'When that time comes, I'll be ready,' Steve said grimly. He raised the Winchester slightly, his finger hard against the trigger, ready if either of the men decided to make a move for his gun.

Apparently neither of the gunmen was prepared to take that chance. Without another backward glance, they pushed their horses through the water, finally climbing up the opposite bank before riding into the distance.

Steve waited until they had disappeared into the shimmering heat haze, then turned the stallion and rode back to the wagons. He found them moving painfully slowly over the smooth alkali.

The men were having a difficult time keeping the horses on the move. There had been very little water for the past two days and the irritating alkali had worked its way into their hoofs, burning the flesh.

Disforth gave him a quick glance as he reined up.

'Find anythin'?' he called.

Steve raised an arm. 'The river is about two miles away. There's an opening in this rockwall where you can get the wagons through a couple at a time.'

The wagon-master nodded. 'That's the best news I've had today. I reckoned we were lost.'

'You're some twenty or so miles south o' the main trail but the river looks safe enough to ford. Trouble is, I ran into a couple of hired gunmen there. They work for some *hombre* called Casson, reckons he owns all o' the land from the river clear to Yellow Buttes. They mean to kill anyone they claim is trespassing on that land.'

'Casson?'

'You know him?'

Grimness showed in every line of Disforth's hard features. 'Ed Casson. Sure I've heard of him. Came out here ten years ago with a band o' killers from somewhere along the border. Took over most o' the land and claimed he'd bought it from the government. What really happened was that he got some crooked lawyer in Yellow Buttes to come up with some fake documents and now he enforces his claim with guns.'

'And you still intend to drive through to Yellow Buttes?'

'Too damned right, I do. We fought off those murderin' Cherokee and we'll do the same to Casson's killers.'

'I still think you're a fool. One man might make it without bein' seen but these wagons are a sittin' target. And takin' on fifty professional gunfighters

34

ain't the same as fightin' a bunch of Indians.'

'We've got no other option open to us. We've come too far to go back and if we're to cross the mountains into California before the winter sets in, we can't afford to make any detours.'

'All right. But once we're over that river, keep all o' the wagons close together. Anyone falls out and they're finished.' Steve meant his words to be a warning and saw from the other's face that they had been taken as such.

By the time all of the wagons had rumbled through the narrow gap in the rocks and reached the wide stretch of open ground bordering the river, the daylight was fading quickly. The sun dropped behind the outlying border of the mountain range, leaving only a diminishing red glow in the heavens.

Steve rode slowly along the train looking for Disforth, but a sudden call from one of the wagons brought him to a halt. Melanie Ridgeway leaned down from the seat. There was a tall, grey-haired man sitting beside her, holding the reins loosely in his hands.

'Does Mister Disforth intend we should cross the river in darkness?' she asked anxiously.

'Could be,' Steve replied. 'There'll be some moonlight but it might be better to wait until morning.' In the forefront of his mind was the thought that, not only might there be some of Casson's men waiting for them on the other side, but the Cherokee might still be trailing them, just waiting for another chance to launch an attack.

The idea of being caught in the middle between these two factions, while trying a river crossing, was one he didn't like. If they made camp on this more open ground, they had a far better chance of defending themselves and there was the possibility that Ed Casson's bunch would not make their play until they were over the river and on his land.

'We've heard there could be big trouble once we cross this river,' her father put in solemnly. 'Is that right?'

'It's true he's threatened to stop any wagon trains crossing that range, which he claims is his,' Steve replied, choosing his words carefully, not wanting to alarm Melanie and her father. 'Not knowin' the man, I can't say what he'll do. We'll just have to face that problem when it comes.'

At that moment Disforth came riding along the train, indicating they were to form themselves into a big circle and make camp there for the night. Evidently, Steve thought, he had been thinking along the same lines as himself. While the wagons were taking up their defensive positions, Steve drew the wagon-master to one side.

'You got somethin' on your mind?' Disforth asked in a low voice when they were out of earshot of the others. 'If it's Ed Casson and his gunslingers—'

'Not them. I reckon Casson will wait until he sees whether his warning has frightened us off before he starts anythin'. I'm reckoning that those Cherokee are still behind us, just waitin' for the chance to hit us again. It ain't like them to let us slip through their fingers after we killed so many of their braves.'

Disforth rubbed his chain thoughtfully. His fingers made a scratching sound that was clearly audible. 'Mebbe you're right, even though we've seen nothin' of 'em since that night attack.'

'If they are gettin' ready for another attack, it'll come tonight. There'll be plenty o' moonlight and this might be their last chance. Somehow, I don't think they'll wait until we're on Casson's spread. They're no fools. The last thing they'll want is all o' Casson's crew huntin' them down.'

'I'll have men posted to keep watch on the camp.'

'Do that. In the meantime, I'll ride back a little way along our trail and keep an eye open for 'em.'

CHAPTER III

DANGEROUS CROSSING

Even in the semi-darkness, the trail taken by the heavy wagons was readily discernible. The moon was now approaching its third quarter but with no clouds in the sky, it still provided enough light for Steve to pick out details for several miles.

By the time he had ridden more than five miles from where the train was camped, he was coming to the conclusion that he had been mistaken. Nothing moved on the wide alkali flats. There were innumerable shadows cast by large clumps of rock but these were all shadows that had a right to be there.

Some distance ahead of him were the tall escarpments, black masses of darkness stretched across the eastern horizon. If the Cherokee were still trailing them, he guessed that it was there they would gather before riding out to follow the clear trail towards the distant river.

Now he reined the stallion to a halt, his eyes three quarters lidded to keep out the moonlight. Here he could see all there was to see, clear to the towering escarpments. Rolling a cigarette, he lit it, pondering on his next move. There were still plenty of hours of darkness left before dawn, plenty of time for the enemy to race their ponies and hit the wagon train before daylight.

The minutes passed slowly and still nothing disturbed the eternal silence of the flats. Then, in the distance, something moved. It was nothing more than a vague, indistinct blur but he knew instinctively what it was. He had not been wrong. The faint cloud of dust told him the Indians were moving quickly and there were more of them than he had reckoned with. Sometime since that last attack, they had been reinforced by others.

Swiftly, almost without thinking, he turned his mount and walked it slowly towards a large butte fifty yards from the edge of the trail. He instinctively refrained from riding quickly, knowing that the Cherokee had sharp eyes and any quick movement would be readily picked out.

In the long shadow of the butte, he waited patiently until he was able to see the advancing group clearly. He judged there were at least forty Cherokee in the group and there was no doubt as to their intentions. This time, they meant to completely overwhelm the defenders among those wagons.

Taking the rifle from its scabbard, he sighted it carefully on the leading riders. He was taking a big chance, hoping to draw a few of them after him.

Once they recognized there was only one man lying in ambush, the main band would continue along the trail.

Gently, he squeezed the trigger, saw the leading Cherokee suddenly lurch as the slug hit him. Throwing out his arms, the brave slid sideways into the dust, rolling directly under the hoofs of the ponies coming up swiftly behind.

Waiting only to fire a second shot that took another of the enemy in the neck, he thrust the Winchester back into the scabbard, wheeled his mount and kicked it hard in the flanks, heading away from the trail. Several whooping yells erupted behind him and risking a quick glance over his shoulder, he saw four of the braves abruptly detach themselves from the rest, spurring their palominos after him.

Lead hummed close to his shoulder as several shots rang out. Another bullet drummed over his head as he pushed himself flat over the stallion's neck. He knew it was not going to be easy to outrun those palominos and the most he could hope for was to stay ahead of them until he could find some kind of cover.

Ahead of him, the ground still seemed absolutely featureless, but then his keen gaze spotted a narrow line of shadow where the land fell sharply away, dropping steeply towards a stretch of much lower region. Swiftly, he spurred his mount towards it. Behind him, the Cherokee were less than a quarter of a mile away.

The descent was far steeper than he had anticipated, an almost sheer drop of thirty feet. Leaning

40

back in the saddle, he put the stallion to it. For a moment, he thought the animal was going to shy away but then it went over the edge, its forelegs straight. Alkali and small stones accompanied him as he reached the bottom.

Without pausing, he slid from the saddle and ran for a thick tangle of thorny mesquite, throwing himself down behind it. Within seconds, the Colts held rock steady in his hands as he thrust his gaze through the flooding moonlight, he waited for the first of the braves to appear.

They showed as a quartet of dark shadows on the high lip of the shelving drop-off, reining up their mounts as they scanned the ground below them. All held their rifles ready. For a moment, Steve held himself completely motionless, steadying his elbows on the gritty ground. Then he thrust himself to his knees, jerking up the Colts in a single, fluid motion.

Swiftly, he fired off several shots. Two of the Cherokee dropped instantly, their bodies rolling limply down the slope. The third brought up his rifle swiftly, firing in almost the same instant. The whining shriek of the ricochet a couple of feet away was echoed by two more shots from the guns in Steve's hands.

The brave swayed, struggled to hold himself upright, then toppled back, out of sight. Before Steve could bring his guns to bear on the fourth man, the other had slid from the saddle and dropped out of sight.

Twisting onto his side, Steve rapidly thrust fresh shells into the Colts. He knew the Cherokee was out

41

there somewhere, waiting for him to make a mistake. Turning his head slowly, he scanned the region around him. There was scarcely any cover and he knew he was effectively pinned down. His mount was still there, standing a few yards away, but he doubted he could reach it without getting a bullet in the back.

Sucking in a deep breath, he lay flat, keeping his gaze on the long ridge, waiting for his adversary to make a move. Tension crackled in the chill air that lay over the flats. He knew it was a case of who could outwait the other, and all the time that main band would be closing the gap on the wagon train.

He swung his gaze to his right. Had there been a movement there, or had he simply imagined it? There was nothing there now, but he was a man who trusted his own instincts. Slowly, he removed his hat. Holding it by the brim, he tossed it quickly to his right.

The rifle shot came almost immediately, the slug kicking up a spurt of dust where his hat had fallen. Rolling onto his shoulder, he sent two shots hammering towards the large rock twenty yards away. The first slug struck the rock and went howling into the distance. The second was followed by a coughing grunt and then silence.

Knowing it could be a ruse, he waited for a full five minutes, then pushed himself slowly to his feet. He went forward cautiously, holding the Colt ready. The Cherokee brave lay on his back, half hidden behind the boulder. There was a neat hole in his chest and his eyes stared sightlessly at the moon.

After checking that there would be no more trouble from the other three, he whistled to the stallion and climbed back into the saddle, heading swiftly in the direction of the river. He deliberately avoided the trail the wagon train had taken, riding across the flats parallel and east of it.

The racketing din of gunfire reached him when he was still almost a mile away. Evidently the men Disforth had posted around the camp had not been taken totally by surprise and were giving a good account of themselves. But against that number of Cherokee, they were completely outnumbered.

Cutting across the alkali, he had come upon the river on top of the high rocks overlooking the bank some thirty feet below. The camp lay to his left, only just visible. Stabbing lances of gunflame showed in the dimness among the wagons drawn up in a tight circle. Others came from the bottom of the rocks just below him.

This time, it seemed the Cherokee had changed their tactics. Their usual mode of attack, racing their mounts around the wagons, had previously resulted in a large number of casualties. Now they were more cautious, secreting themselves among the rocks where there was plenty of cover.

Not only were the Indians using rifles but, from what he could see, they had also employed a number of fire arrows. Two of the wagons were blazing fiercely, yet in spite of the rifle fire pouring into the camp, several woman were struggling to douse the flames, heedless of their own danger.

Ducking low, Steve moved across the narrow plateau, crouching down at the far end. Running his gaze over the scene, he made a rough estimate of the enemy. He judged that about half of them lay dead among the boulders but that still left around a score of them and there seemed no indication they intended giving up the fight.

Crawling to his right, he came up against a massive spur of rock, far higher than himself. Here, he was able to stand while still remaining under cover. There was a small outjutting ledge of stone on the side of the rock and, resting the barrel of the Winchester on it, he peered along the sights.

Squeezing the trigger gently, he saw the shot go home. The brave half turned as the impact of the slug threw him against the rocks. For a moment, he seemed to stare directly at the spot where Steve stood, but he was seeing nothing. Slumping forward, his limp body careered over the ledge, hitting the ground twelve feet below.

Deftly, Steve swung the rifle slightly, drew the sights on another and then a third. It was several seconds before the Cherokee recognized where the gunfire was coming from. Completely exposed to their rear, they flattened themselves behind any cover they could find.

A moment later, Disforth's booming voice came from below. 'It's Calladine. He's up there among those rocks behind these critters. We've got 'em pinned down from two sides.'

Regardless of their danger, a group of men burst out of the camp and ran forward. Pulling his Colts from their holsters, Steve gave the men covering fire. Ten minutes later, it was all over. Only three of the

Cherokee succeeded in reaching their ponies, spurring into the distance.

'Reckon they won't be troublin' us again,' Disforth called loudly as Steve rode into the camp. 'Seems they got a lot more than they bargained for.'

Stepping down, Steve loosened the cinch and took off the saddle. 'Did you lose many men?' he asked shortly, glancing about him.

'Three killed and five wounded. We also lost a couple of wagons that were burned out. Considerin' how many o' those critters were in that bunch, I'd say we got off pretty lightly.'

Nodding, Steve said soberly, 'That attack was nothin' compared with what you'll face out yonder on the other side o' the river. If Casson's men don't hit you when you try the crossin', it's a sure bet they will before you've gone ten miles.'

Sitting tensely on the wooden seat, Herb Wisley twisted the reins tightly around both hands, clutching them with white-knuckled fingers. Beside him, his wife sat with her back as stiff as a ramrod, staring straight in front of her. The expression on her face told him nothing of the thoughts that were running through her mind at that moment.

Both of them, and the two children, had come through the Indian attacks unscathed. In the heat of the fighting, there had been little time in which to be afraid. But the sight of the swiftly flowing river in front of them was daunting and the knowledge that there might be a band of gunmen waiting on the other side did nothing to alleviate their fears.

Theirs was the first wagon due to make the crossing. Calladine had ridden across only a few minutes earlier and now sat his mount on the far bank, alert for any sign of trouble. Disforth rode up from the rear. Leaning sideways in the saddle, he called, 'You ready, Herb?'

Running his tongue over lips suddenly gone dry, Wisley forced a nod. 'As ready as we'll ever be, I guess.'

'Good. Just keep a tight hold on the reins and keep those horses moving straight forward. The river seems sufficiently shallow for them to keep their feet.'

For a moment, Wisley still hesitated. Then, reaching down, Martha lifted the long whip and brought it down on the backs of the horses. Straining forward in the traces, the animals moved down the smoothly shelving bank and into the water.

Almost at once, the current caught them and the wagon swayed precariously, then miraculously righted itself. One of the children uttered a high-pitched yell before lapsing into silence. Clenching his teeth, Wisley let the horses have their heads.

In the middle, the water rose almost to the top of the wheels but still they managed to remain upright.

'You're past the worst of it.' Steve's reassuring voice reached them from the far bank. Straining mightily, the horses hauled the heavy wagon through the water onto the far side.

Behind them, the others were crossing. Steve watched them tensely. Even though the river was sufficiently shallow, even in the middle, for the horses and oxen to maintain their footing, the surging currents were capricious. They could strike without warning and from almost any direction. Three men on horseback were in the water, ready with lariats in case any of the wagons went over, but danger could strike so quickly that even this precaution might prove inadequate.

An hour passed and only one wagon remained to cross. Steve experienced a little stab of apprehension as he noticed Melanie seated beside her father. The horses seemed particularly skittish as Matt Ridgeway guided them towards the water's edge. A moment later, they were in the river.

Everything went well at first but then, for no reason, the two leading horses lunged to an abrupt stop. Ridgeway flicked the whip across their backs but still they refused to budge. Behind them, the water was swirling swiftly against the side of the wagon, mounting higher against the wooden boxes slung along it, threatening to tilt it over onto its side.

Without thinking, Steve urged his own mount forward. He waved an arm towards one of the riders already in the river. 'Grab those reins,' he yelled harshly. Thankfully, the man understood immediately. Even as Steve came alongside the leading horse, the man caught at the other. Together, they hauled at the horses, dragging them reluctantly forward.

From the edge of his vision, a split second before he heard Melanie's cry of alarm, Steve saw the wagon lurch and tilt sideways under the rising pressure of the current. Then, seemingly out of nowhere, a second rider had approached, whirling his lariat over his head.

The noose dropped neatly over the wooden post. Swiftly, the lariat snapped taut as the rider looped it around his pommel. Backing a couple of feet, he managed to haul the wagon upright. Five minutes later, Melanie and her father were safely across.

Glancing down at Steve, Melanie said softly, 'I think you saved our lives this time, Steve.'

Nodding, he replied, 'We were lucky, I guess. Now let's see what this *hombre* Casson has in store for us.'

Disforth had already formed the wagons into a tight line. Now he waved his arm. His shout could be heard all the way along the train. 'We're headin' west. Keep close together and have your rifles ready.'

CHAPTER IV

YELLOW BUTTES

Thirty miles west of the wagon train, Ed Casson stood on the ranch porch and turned over in his mind the news his two hirelings had brought him the previous day. It had disturbed him greatly although at the time he had tried hard not to show it. He had no compunction against killing all of the people in those wagons and taking everything they carried.

This was his land and he had fought long and hard in the past to keep it. Knowing he had Sheriff Trenton in Yellow Buttes completely under his thumb, there was little fear anyone would ever discover how he had come by it. Yet the nagging worries remained in his mind.

He had guessed that the stranger who had ridden into Yellow Buttes some months earlier was a Federal marshal, poking his nose into things along this stretch of the frontier. Even though the other had been asking questions about Cal Forden and his own name had not been mentioned, it had been clear that the Federal authorities were now taking too big an interest in what was going on in these parts.

Only the fact that Forden had arranged for that marshal to be killed soon after he ridden into Calder Wells had eased some of the tension. But he had known all along that, sooner or later, other lawmen would come, determined to find out what had happened in that town and this time it could be anyone riding with these wagon trains, working in secret.

Since that time, he had ordered his men to keep a sharp eye on any homesteaders moving west along the north trail. So far, no one had pulled out of the trains and headed towards either Yellow Buttes or Calder Wells but he could not afford to relax his vigilance. Now there was another; one intent on crossing the river onto his land, taking a trail that would pass within ten miles of Yellow Buttes.

To his way of thinking that could only mean that some lawman was travelling with this train intent on making trouble for both himself and Forden. Not that he cared at all about what happened to the other rancher. Indeed, it would suit him fine if Forden was either arrested or killed.

There had always been tension between him and the other man. Several of his steers had gone over the hill where the boundary ran between these two biggest spreads in this region north and south around Yellow Buttes.

With Forden out of the way, there would be little to prevent him taking over the entire Lazy T land. But if the Federal authorities were to come and start asking awkward questions, that was an entirely different matter. Somehow, he had to find out if there was anyone travelling with that wagon train who was something more than a settler hoping to begin a new life in California.

That left him with only two choices. Either he could follow his instincts and send his men out with orders to eliminate everyone on that wagon train before they got very far, or he could allow them to pass and see if anyone left it and headed for Yellow Buttes. Thinking it over, he reckoned that it would be far easier to deal with a stranger in town where there would be nowhere for him to run, than to run the risk of him getting away during a gunfight with the settlers.

Going out onto the porch, he called to the two men standing just inside the doorway of the adjacent bunkhouse. The foreman, Seth Yarrow, tossed his half-smoked cigarette-butt into the dust, ground it out with his heel, and walked over, followed by Miguel Dominguez, the Mexican.

'That stranger you found near the river, did he look like a Federal marshal, maybe one without a star?' he demanded roughly.

Yarrow pursed his thin lips. 'Weren't no doubt he's a gunslick, probably one hired by the wagon-master to protect the train.'

Casson switched his gaze to Dominguez. 'What do you think?'

The other spread his hands in a gesture that could mean anything. 'To me, Señor Casson, he looked like the kind of two-bit gunman you'll find in any town

51

along the frontier. A man who sells his gun to the highest bidder.'

Butting in, Yarrow said softly, 'I reckon he's the only man riding with that train who's dangerous. The rest are just farmers and townsfolk from back East. They'll make a fight of it to protect what they've got but you've no need to worry. With all the men you have, it'll all be over in an hour and—'

'No!' Casson spat the word out. 'I've been thinkin' and that's not the way I want it. Let them come. Once they get close to Yellow Buttes, I want them watched all the way, day and night. You understand?'

'Just what have you got in mind, boss?' Yarrow enquired. 'If you allow this train to cross your land it won't be long before others come. They'll rustle your beef and tear up the pastures.'

Dominguez nodded his agreement. 'And once Forden hears of this, he'll reckon you've gone soft. That could mean trouble.'

'Leave me to deal with Cal Forden,' Casson snapped. 'Just make sure my orders are carried out. As soon as they're off my land at Yellow Buttes, they'll be drivin' across his and it'll be up to him what to do with 'em.'

Turning on his heel, he went back into the ranch. Pausing at the door, he turned and signalled to Yarrow to follow him. Once inside, he closed the door and motioned the other to a chair.

Seating himself opposite, he opened the drawer and brought out a bottle and two glasses. 'You've been my foreman for quite some time, Seth,' he said, pouring whiskey into one of the glasses and sliding it across to the other.

'Ten years,' Yarrow agreed.

Nodding, Casson went on, 'You're the only man I've got I can trust. The others are just hired gunslingers who'd ride on if they got a better offer from Forden. I want you to do somethin' for me.'

'Sure.' Yarrow tossed half of his drink down in one swallow.

'Reckon you recall that stranger who rode into Calder Wells some months back, the one your brother killed.'

Yarrow's lips twisted into what was meant to be a smile. 'From what I hear, he was askin' too many questions about Cal Forden.' His eyes, normally cold and emotionless, were now narrowed in an expression of curiosity.

'My guess is he was a Federal marshal and even though he's dead, that could spell trouble, not only for Forden, but for me.'

Resting his elbows on the table, the foreman stared down at the whiskey swirling in his glass. 'You're figgerin' there might be more headed this way, hopin' to find out what happened to him?'

'That's right. Only this time, they'll send someone we don't suspect. My guess is it'll be someone ridin' with one o' these wagon trains. From what you've told me, it could be that *hombre* you met at the river. Seems strange to me that these settlers are travellin' this far south of the usual route they take. Maybe he's made some kind o' deal with whoever is leading that train and he intends to slip away from the others and ride into Yellow Buttes the first chance he gets.'

Finishing his drink, Casson set the empty glass down on the desk. There was a crafty expression on his hard features. 'But two can play at that game. I want you to follow that train and I don't want you to be seen. If that *hombre*, or anyone else, makes a move towards Yellow Buttes, I want to know about it. You got that?'

'You want me to go alone?'

Running a finger down his cheek, Casson thought for a moment. 'No, take Dominguez with you. If I'm right, this *hombre* will slip away from the train just as soon as they're clear of my territory. Should that happen, send Dominguez back here with the word. You trail this man and find out where he goes, who he talks to. I'll do the rest.'

Half an hour later, Yarrow and Dominguez rode out of the wide courtyard, taking the narrow trail towards the eastern edge of the spread. They rode swiftly, but cautiously. It would be easy to spot the wagons but there was the chance that one or more of the men might be riding ahead.

Yarrow had already decided that the wagon train would take the shortest and quickest way across the wide grasslands. Having been given that warning, it was highly unlikely they would deviate from that route. Accordingly, the two men rode well away from the trail, keeping far to the south.

By dusk, dark clouds had moved in from the south, bringing a steady downpour. Leaning forward into the slanting rain, they rode into the low, wooded hills. Just a few minutes earlier, they had spotted the long string of small dots some five miles distant, edging slowly along, one behind each other.

'Reckon they've made good time since fordin' the river, *amigo*,' Dominguez remarked casually, shaking the rain from the brim of his sombrero. 'They sure ain't heedin' the warning we gave 'em. If we had the rest of the men with us, we could take them all.'

'You heard what the boss said. We leave 'em alone. We just keep 'em in sight until they reach the fork into Yellow Buttes.'

'And then let Cal Forden have the pleasure of takin' everything they've got.' Sarcasm and disappointment edged the half-breed's tone. 'It wouldn't surprise me if there ain't gold in some o' them wagons.'

'Casson's got his reasons for letting 'em across,' Yarrow muttered shortly. Through a gap in the trees, he could still just make out the distant wagons. They appeared to have swung into a circle now. From the way they were moving, he reckoned they intended to camp for the night.

Swinging from the saddle, he said, 'We'll camp here. They won't go on once it gets dark. We can pick 'em up again in the mornin'.'

'Do we have to sleep cold?'

Yarrow threw a swift glance around the small clearing. Even with the overhanging branches, the rain was still managing to seep through. He recognized the danger of lighting a fire but those men would be expecting to be attacked in force. Any men they had posted as lookouts would be concentrating on the trail west.

Finally, he said, 'I reckon it'll be safe to light a fire.'

Squatting beside the flames, feeling the heat beating at his sodden clothing until they steamed, Yarrow washed down the food with scalding hot coffee brewed over the fire. Even though he could see the logic behind Casson's decision, he still considered it to be the wrong one.

They had no proof there were any lawmen heading for Yellow Buttes and Calder Wells. Maybe that was all in Casson's mind, seeing trouble where none existed. What his companion had said earlier was almost certainly true. Some of those settlers would be carrying gold with them.

He still had that thought in his mind when he rolled himself into his blankets, cursing the rain, which now came down on them in large drops from the overhead branches.

Riding slightly ahead of the train, Steve felt a deep sense of worry and uncertainty running riot through his mind. They had driven slowly across the rich grassland for two days and still there had been no sight of Casson's men. Every moment, he had anticipated a concerted attack against them, but it had never materialized.

Either Casson was deliberately luring them into a trap or, for some reason known only to himself, had decided to do nothing. Knowing the type of men these cattle barons were, it did not seem possible that the other meant to allow them to cross his land unmolested. Yet as far as he could judge, the trail into Yellow Buttes, where the river formed the western boundary of this spread, lay only a few miles ahead.

Slowing his mount, he waited until the first of the wagons passed by. Glancing down at him from the wagon, Melanie noticed the deep frown on his face and said, 'You look worried, Steve. You got something on your mind?'

He forced a wry smile. 'Nothin' for you to worry about. It just don't seem right to me that those two gunmen should warn us against crossing this spread, yet we've seen neither hair nor hide of Casson's men.'

'Surely that's something to be glad about.'

'It might be if only I could figger out the reason for it.'

Before he could say anything further, Disforth rode up. He gave Steve a sharp, enigmatic glance as he said, 'Yellow Buttes is about fifteen miles to the north of here. You still intend leavin' the train and goin' to that helltown?'

'I'm afraid I've got no choice. This is somethin' I have to do. If I don't find out anythin' there, I'll join you further along the trail.'

'You're a damned fool. Go there and you'll only be puttin' yourself in danger.'

'When do you intend to leave?' Melanie asked. There was a little tremor in her voice, which Steve noticed at once.

Steve squinted at the sun where it was now sinking behind the range of hills in the distance. 'We should reach the trail into Yellow Buttes in another hour or so. I'll pull out as soon as it gets dark.'

Staring straight ahead, Melanie said softly, 'Be careful. If your brother has been killed, whoever did it might be expecting someone to come, someone with vengeance on his mind.'

'And if you don't find any evidence in Yellow Buttes that your brother was killed there?' Disforth asked. 'Are you goin' to spend the rest o' your life lookin'?'

'Then I guess I'll just ride on to Calder Wells and ask around there,' Steve retorted bitterly. 'Of one thing I am sure. Somebody murdered him and I don't aim to rest until I've hunted his killer down.'

Disforth spread his hands in exasperation. 'I reckon there ain't no point tryin' to talk sense into a man intent on vengeance.' He touched spurs to his mount and rode on towards the front of the train.

Turning his head, Steve looked across at the girl. 'Do you think I'm wrong, Melanie?' he asked.

He saw her hesitate for a moment. Then she shook her head. 'Sometimes there are things a man has to do no matter how senseless it may seem to others, otherwise it eats into his soul until he has nothing left.'

Nodding his thanks at her understanding, Steve turned the stallion's head, his keen glance now surveying the land ahead. Here, it was possible to see for miles in every conceivable direction. Yet if this was ranchland, why had they seen no one? Certainly, this spread was so big that any herd of cattle Ed Casson owned could be miles away.

But knowing the animosity that often existed between rival ranchers, why were men not patrolling the boundaries? There was something here that didn't sit right. He turned his head to check on the lumbering wagons at the rear of the train.

Far off to the south there was a sudden movement. Had he not caught it with averted vision, he might have missed it completely. Far off in the distance, so far they were barely distinguishable from the background, he made out the two riders close to the horizon. Swiftly, he scanned the area for any more, but there was nothing.

Wheeling his mount, he rode quickly towards the head of the train until he was alongside Disforth. 'We're bein' trailed,' he said sharply.

'You certain?' The wagon-master pulled the sorrel to a sliding halt.

Steve pointed. 'I spotted 'em a minute ago. Whoever they are they seem to be keepin' their distance.'

Disforth squinted into the deepening twilight. For a moment, he saw nothing. Then he gave a brief nod. 'I see them but there can't be more than two or three. They couldn't give us any trouble.'

Grimly, Steve said, 'Somehow, I doubt if it's the train they're after.'

'Then what?' Disforth gave him a sharp glance.

'I think it's me they're trailin'. That could explain why Casson hasn't attacked us even though we are crossin' his land. My brother was tryin' to get evidence against these big cattlemen who're running this territory. Could be someone got wise to him and that was why he was killed. Now they figure someone has been sent to find out exactly what happened.'

Disforth pressed his lips into a tight line. 'So you think they reckon you might be another marshal?'

'It makes sense, unless you've got another suggestion as to why this train hasn't been attacked before now.'

'Nope. I guess it's the only explanation that makes any sense. But if you're right, you'll be headin' into a whole heap o' trouble. Like I told you when we set out, there ain't no law and order here, only the law o' the gun. How do you figger you'll get anyone to talk to you?'

'Somebody knows somethin'. Maybe those two back yonder on the trail. My guess is they mean to follow me once I leave this train.'

'And you intend to let them?' There was a note of incredulity in the older man's voice.

'That's right. I'm sure they're the two I met at the river. Maybe they'll lead me to my brother's killer.'

Less than an hour later, the leading wagons forded the narrow river that marked the boundary of the Casson spread. Here, a narrow trail wound away to the north. Night had fallen swiftly and now there was no sign of the men who had been following them but Steve knew they were still there, that they had almost certainly closed the gap.

As he made to ride out, Disforth rode up and held out his hand. 'Take care, Calladine,' he said throatily. 'I hope you find what you're lookin' for.'

Shaking hands, Steve said harshly, 'If not, I'll try to make it back to the trail and ride on with you to Calder Wells.'

'You'll be welcome.'

Jerking on the reins, Steve put the stallion to the narrow trail. Very soon, the wagon train was lost to sight, vanishing into the darkness. Ahead of him, the trail angled towards a low ridge topped with first-growth pine. He rode swiftly, putting his mount to the steep upgrade, not slowing until he was among the trees.

Here, he pulled the stallion off the trail, shielded from sight by the thick undergrowth. By now he had no doubt that he would be followed. Quite clearly, this rancher Casson wanted to know who he was and why he was here. Pulling up the collar of his jacket, he built himself a smoke and settled down to wait.

Twenty minutes passed and still he heard nothing. Had he been mistaken? Was it possible that Casson was interested only in the wagon train and had lured it to the very edge of his spread so that if there was any law in this territory, he might be able to put the blame on his old enemy Cal Forden?

Deciding to wait no longer, he touched spurs to the stallion's flanks, then hauled back sharply as a sudden movement caught his eye. A chill went through him as he realized he had almost given himself away. The rider was less than twenty feet away, a dark shadow on the opposite side of the trail.

The other was deliberately riding through the trees, making scarcely a sound. Through narrow eyes, Steve tried to establish the other's identity. After a few seconds, he was sure it was the tall killer he had met at the river. There was no sign of the smaller man who had accompanied him on that occasion.

Tensely, Steve waited until the other had passed out of sight. Clearly the gunman was a professional killer, a man who took no chances. For a full five minutes, Steve remained where he was, feeling the tension mount within him like a coiled spring.

Either that man was riding alone, or his partner was riding some distance behind in case of trouble. When there was no further sound or movement, he edged the stallion down towards the edge of the trail. Every sense alert, he probed the darkness in front of him and behind. Against men such as these, he knew that death could be very close, could come at any moment.

A little while later, the trees thinned and he was forced to move more slowly, knowing Casson's man could be lying in wait for him. Then, some fifty yards away, he glimpsed the other, now riding more swiftly.

Here was more open, hilly country and now the moon had risen, making it easier for the other to spot him. A quick glance over his shoulder told Steve there was no one on his tail. Obviously only one of the men had followed him from the wagon train. Evidently any others would have ridden back to Casson's place to inform him of what had happened.

Keeping into the shadows thrown by the hills, Steve maintained his distance. From the way the man kept glancing along the trail at his back, he guessed that the other was puzzled. Once or twice, he pulled his mount to a halt, turning in the saddle to scan the terrain behind him.

The second time this happened, he evidently made up his mind that by now Steve was somewhere ahead of him for he put his mount into a fast run, kicking up a clearly visible trail of dust.

Knowing he had to keep the other in sight, Steve

gigged his own mount to a fast run, moving as often as possible into the deep shadows. As he rode, he turned over in his mind what to do once he hit Yellow Buttes. The first thing that man ahead of him would do would be to alert any of his friends in the town, giving his description to all of the outlaws and gunslammers who were in on the lawless activities going on in this territory.

Somehow, he doubted if he would find anyone who would willingly give him the information he needed. From what Disforth had told him, there would be no hope of the sheriff co-operating with him. Whoever he was, this so-called lawman would be in cahoots with both Casson and Forden.

The only choice left to him would be to keep his eyes and ears open and watch his back every second.

An hour later, he topped a low rise where the trail ran straight on into the town directly below him, half a mile away. Lights showed in most of the buildings along either side of the single street. What was clearly the sheriff's office and jailhouse stood at the end nearest to him. Directly opposite it was a tall, three storey building with a broken sign outside, hanging lop-sidedly above the entrance.

Several of the townsfolk were out on the streets and he guessed there were many more inside the three saloons spaced out almost evenly along the left-hand side.

Slowly, he moved the big stallion forward down the slope. Then, just as he drew level with the sheriff's office, the door swung open and someone stepped out onto the sidewalk. Even in the shadows, Steve recognized the man instantly.

Inwardly, he felt little surprise. He was the one he had met at the river, the one who had passed him on the trail. Evidently word was already being passed on about him.

As he swung down from the saddle, the man glanced up quickly. For a moment, there was an expression of startled shock on the other's face. Then he recovered himself quickly and made to move towards the narrow alley running alongside the jail.

He halted abruptly as Steve said quietly, 'I guess you must have missed me along the trail, mister. Any reason why you were followin' me?'

'I weren't followin' anyone.' There was a note of suppressed cunning in his tone. 'I come into town nearly every night. What you do ain't no business o' mine.'

'No? Seems to me I recall you threatened to kill me if we ever met again.'

'Mebbe I will but I ain't going to draw on you right now. I can wait. We don't take too kindly to strangers in Yellow Buttes. Could be someone else will get you before I do. One thing's for sure. If you're here lookin' for trouble, you won't ride out again.'

Before Steve could say anything more, the other spun sharply on his heels and darted into the alley, leaving the threat hanging in the air.

Steve waited until the sound of his footsteps had died away before hitching the stallion to the rail. Stepping up onto the boardwalk, he pushed open the door of the sheriff's office and went inside.

In the light of the lamp on the desk, he made out the short, florid-faced man who sat there. Another younger man lounged against the wall on the far side, a cigarette dangling from his lips. Both looked up in obvious surprise as he entered.

'You the sheriff here?' Steve asked tersely.

For a moment, the other's eyes swung towards the guns at Steve's waist. Then he glanced up, his eyes narrowed. 'That's right, stranger. I'm Sheriff Trenton. Somethin' I can do for you?' The other's tone implied that he didn't like the way he was being addressed.

From the edge of his vision, Steve saw the deputy push himself slightly away from the wall, his right hand hanging loosely near his gun.

'That man who just left, who is he?'

'Seth Yarrow. He's Ed Casson's ranch foreman. What's your business with him?'

Steve gave a grim smile. 'I only met him once before when he warned me off Casson's spread but since he trailed me all the way here and the first person in Yellow Buttes he speaks to is you, I figure he's got some interest in me and I aim to find out what it is.'

Trenton leaned back in his chair, his hands flat on the desk in front of him. He seemed to be debating what to say but finally he said, 'I reckon you should know that I'm the law in Yellow Buttes and I don't aim to have any trouble. Whatever's between you and Yarrow, you can settle it outside o' town. In the meantime, if you intend stayin' in town, I'd advise you to walk carefully.'

'Now why should I do that, Sheriff?' Steve saw the other flinch slightly at the veiled threat in his voice.

Before Trenton could speak, the deputy spoke up. 'You'll do that, mister, because at the first hint o' trouble, you'll either find yourself in one o' those cells back there or, if you're real lucky, we'll just run you outta town. Mister Casson don't like men walkin' the streets o' Yellow Buttes that he knows nothin' about.'

'Thanks for the warnin'.' The note of sarcasm in Steve's voice did not go unnoticed by the two men. 'I guess that's the hotel just across the street. Reckon I can get a bed there for the night.'

Turning on his heel, he went outside, closing the door behind him. The noise and music was still spilling out of the saloons and he guessed it would go on for several more hours. Leading the stallion across the street, he pushed open the hotel door and stepped inside.

For a moment, he thought there was no one around. Then, as he reached the desk, there was a sudden movement and a small, balding man stepped into sight from somewhere at the side.

'You got a room for the night?' Steve asked.

'Sure, but—' Breaking off, the proprietor leaned forward a little, studying Steve closely. 'You ain't one o' Casson's men, are you?'

Steve shook his head, noticing that the other seemed suddenly nervous. 'I've just ridden into town. A friend o' mine rode this way a while back. Maybe you remember him, Jim Calladine.'

'Calladine?' For an instant, there was something

66

on the wrinkled features that told Steve the other knew the name. Swallowing hard, his adam's apple bobbing up and down in his throat, he shook his head quickly. 'Afraid I don't know the name.'

'No? It seems to me this is the only hotel in this town and, since I know he came here, this is the only place where he could put up.'

'Maybe he just rode through. We get plenty like that. Men on the run from the law. Men lookin' for jobs with the cattlemen.'

It was obvious to Steve he would get nothing from this man. The other was clearly scared of talking to strangers. 'All right,' he said shortly, 'just give me the key to the room.'

He found the room at the front of the hotel. It was small with a bed, a small cabinet by the wall and a rickety chair in one corner. A jug of water and a basin stood on the cabinet.

Going over to the window, he pressed himself against the wall and looked down into the street below. A minute later, he spotted the figure of the proprietor crossing the street. As he had expected, the other threw a wary glance along the street in both directions and then entered the sheriff's office. Obviously, his movements were being reported back to Trenton.

Satisfied, he turned back into the room, then halted at a soft knock on the door. Drawing one of the Colts from its holster, he moved quickly and silently across the room and jerked the door open, bringing up the gun as he did so.

Then he lowered it as he saw the woman standing

there. He could see little of her features in the dim light. Her white hair was pulled back into a tight bun on the back of her head.

Before he could stop her, she had pushed past him, motioning him to close the door.

'I have to speak to you,' she said in a low voice. 'I was in the back room and heard you ask my husband about a man called Calladine.'

'You know somethin' about him?'

'He stayed here at the hotel about three months ago. I remember him quite clearly. I got the feeling he was some kind of lawman. He was asking about a man called Forden, but I don't know what his interest in him was.'

'Do you know what happened to him?'

He saw her shake her head. 'I know there was talk in town that he was here to make trouble. Sheriff Trenton said he was a wanted killer from somewhere down near the Mexico border. Two of Ed Casson's men rode into town and said they'd swear out a warrant for his arrest.'

'You don't know if he got out o' this town alive, do you?'

'I never heard he'd been killed, but in this town men get themselves killed every day.' As if she had said more than she should, she moved quickly towards the door. 'Don't let anyone know I've spoken to you, not even my husband. He's a good man but like most of the others in Yellow Buttes he has to do as Casson says. And don't trust the sheriff or his deputy. They're both in Casson's pay.'

'Is there anyone in town who might tell me

whether this man got out of here alive?'

The woman paused with her hand around the handle. She was silent for a moment, then said, 'There's only Zeb Wheeler. He's an old man, older than me, and most folk reckon he's touched in the head. Maybe that's why he's stayed alive for so long. But he spends most of his time prowling around the town. Now I must go before my husband gets back.'

'Where do I find this Zeb Wheeler?'

'He has a shack right on the far edge of town.' With these words, the woman left, closing the door softly behind her.

CHAPTER V

DEATH BY NIGHT

Ed Casson was standing by the window when Dominguez rode into the courtyard. From the state of Dominguez's mount, he guessed that the other had ridden hard and fast. Going out onto the porch, he waited until the other alighted and came towards him.

'Well?' he demanded roughly. 'What happened?'

'Just like you said, Señor Casson. That *hombre* left the wagon train the minute they reached the trail into Yellow Buttes.'

Casson nodded, satisfied. So he had not been wrong about this man. Now, more than ever, he was convinced the other was another Federal marshal working incognito. It posed a problem but not one he couldn't deal with.

'Yarrow followed him like I ordered?'

'Si, Señor. They should both be in town by now.'

'Good. Now we know who he is and where he is, it shouldn't be too difficult to deal with him.'

'You want me to get word to Yellow Buttes and have him killed?'

'No. There's nothing to connect me with Calladine's death and I intend it should stay that way. I've had dealin's with the Federal authorities before and I know how they operate. This is goin' just as I planned. It won't be long before Forden gets wind of that train crossin' his land and my guess is he'll send most of his men after it. That's when we hit the Lazy T. Just see to it that all o' the boys are ready as soon as I give the word. We'll wipe him out once and for all.'

Grinning wolfishly, Dominguez turned and made his way across the courtyard to the bunkhouse. Casson watched him go, then took a cigar from his pocket, lit it, and stared out into the night. With Cal Forden out of the way, all of this territory would be his.

By one o' clock in the morning, the entire town seemed deserted. The last of the revellers had left the saloons. As far as Steve could see from the window, only one light showed and that was in the sheriff's office just across the street.

An hour earlier, Trenton and his deputy had stepped out onto the boardwalk. The deputy had taken the side of the street immediately below Steve's room. For a moment, he had stood there, looking up at the windows. Then, both men had moved on into town.

Some time later, they had returned and now only an occasional shadow passed across the office window indicating that possibly both men were still awake.

Steve waited for a little while longer, then went over to the door, opening it quietly. There was no sound inside the hotel and he reckoned both the proprietor and his wife were asleep. Making no sound, he edged down the stairs and into the lobby. As he had hoped, the place was empty and in total darkness.

The street door was locked but fortunately the proprietor had left the key in the lock. A moment later he was outside on the boardwalk, pressing himself hard into the wall as he threw a wary glance across the street. At any moment, he expected the door to be flung open and Trenton to come running out but after a little while, he felt sure neither of the two men had spotted him.

Unhitching the stallion, he led it slowly along the narrow alley until he reached the rear of the hotel. Here, the rough ground had been given over to a cluster of warehouses, all of which stood in silence in the pale wash of moonlight.

Swinging into the saddle, he let his mount pick its way over piles of rocks and patches of coarse grass until he reached the northern end of the town. The proprietor's wife had said that Zeb Wheeler had a shack somewhere in this vicinity and he cast about for some sign of it.

Eventually, he spotted a decrepit hovel stood well away from any other buildings. One of the windows was broken and there was no sign of life about it. He approached cautiously, knowing that some of these old-timers were inclined to shoot at strangers first and then ask questions.

He was less than five yards away when a sudden movement caught his eye. The moonlight glinted off the barrel of a shotgun thrust through the broken window. The barrel was aimed directly at him.

'Stop just where you are, mister, or I'll let you have both barrels.'

Steve reined up sharply, sitting straight in the saddle with his hands well away from his guns where the other could see them. 'Are you Zeb Wheeler?' he asked, keeping his voice low.

'Who wants to know?' There was something in the harsh, wheezing voice that told Steve the other would not hesitate to pull the trigger if he made a wrong move.

'I've been told you might be able to tell me something about a stranger who rode into Yellow Buttes three months ago. Jim Calladine.'

There was a pause, then the voice came again, 'I remember him. What was he to you, stranger?'

'He was my brother. I'm tryin' to find out what happened to him.'

There was a longer pause this time. Then the shotgun was withdrawn and a moment later, the door swung open on protesting hinges.

The man who stepped outside was old, with a white beard and long side whiskers but his eyes were bright and shrewd and he held the weapon rocksteady in his hands. 'All right. Step down and come inside, but no funny moves.'

Steve slid from the saddle and moved slowly towards the oldster, hands held well away from his sides. The other stood a little to one side, then followed him in and closed the door. It was dark inside the shack, but a moment later, there was the scrape of a match and the other lit the lantern on the small wooden table.

'You come here askin' about this fella Calladine.' Wheeler laid the shotgun against the wall near the door. He uttered a cackling laugh. 'I had him figured for a lawman the minute I laid eyes on him. When he started askin' questions about Casson and Forden, I guessed he was probably a Federal marshal.'

'Do you know what happened to him?' Steve persisted.

Without replying, the other crossed to a small cupboard and took out a bottle of whiskey. Tilting it to his lips, he took a couple of deep swallows, grimacing as the raw liquor hit the back of his throat. He offered it to Steve and when the other shook his head, he drank down some more, before placing it on the table.

'Old Zeb knows a lot more o' what goes on in Yellow Buttes than anybody thinks. They reckon I see and hear nothin' but they're wrong. All of 'em. I'm nothin' but a crazy old coot who just spends his time wanderin' around the town. But—'

He seemed on the verge of rambling and Steve interrupted him more sharply than he intended. 'My brother came here askin' questions about Casson and Forden. My guess is that somebody didn't like that so they killed him.'

Wheeler wiped his mouth with the back of his hand. 'Don't know where you heard that, mister. Sure he stayed here for three or four days, pokin' his nose into their business and it's true somebody took a shot at him from one o' the alleys. But he weren't killed here. He rode out o' Yellow Buttes takin' the trail to Calder Wells.'

'You're sure o' that?'

'Course I'm sure. I saw him myself. It were just after sunset. Whether he ever got to Calder Wells or whether he were bushwhacked somewhere along the trail, I don't know.'

The oldster walked across to the window. 'I do know he was alive when he rode out.'

'Did you ever get to talk to him?'

'Sure. It were the same day he rode out. I asked him straight out what he expected to find. I didn't reckon he'd tell me anythin' but I guess he figgered I was different from the others.'

'What did he tell you?'

'Said he'd already got plenty of evidence that apart from bein' behind several hold-ups, both Casson and Forden were runnin' guns to the Indians. He had it all written down in some report he meant to send to the army at Fort Augusta. He said—'

Before Wheeler could complete his sentence a shot rang out, shattering the clinging silence. A second later, the old man fell back, crashing against the low table. Within seconds, Steve had thrust himself forward, sliding the Colts from their holsters. He went down on one knee behind the window, peering out into the faint moonlight.

For a moment, he saw nothing. Then a slight movement at the edge of his vision brought him upright. Swinging the Colt, he loosed off a couple of shots after the running figure, cursing as both bullets missed.

Holstering the gun, he went back to where Wheeler lay sprawled on the floor. Even in the dimness, he made out the spreading stain on the front of the other's shirt. The old man struggled to push himself up, then slumped back with a low, bubbling moan.

When he spoke, pushing the words out through his teeth, the words were barely audible. 'You'd . . . you'd better fork your bronc and ride out o' here, mister. Pretty soon, there'll be all hell let loose and you can be sure they'll frame you for this.'

A spasm of coughing gripped the other's slight frame. Then his lips moved again. 'Do like I say. If you don't, you'll be stretchin' rope by mornin'. There ain't nothin' you can do for me. Now, if you value your life, git!'

A gush of blood came from the corner of his mouth, soaking into his beard. For a moment, his eyes held a spark of life in them. Then they went vacant and his head fell limply to one side.

Getting swiftly to his feet, Steve moved outside, throwing a wary glance in both directions. The street looked utterly deserted but he knew there was a killer somewhere in those shadows and the urge to hunt him down was almost more than he could master. Then a cold calmness took over.

What the old man had said was true. Much of the town would have been alerted by those gunshots. Once Wheeler's body was found and it was discovered his own bed had not been slept in, there would be a posse on his trail. No doubt there would be someone willing to swear they had seen him at this shack.

Swinging up into the saddle, he raked spurs along the stallion's flanks and sent it racing forward into the rough country that lay to the north. If Casson, or someone else, had planned this they had executed it well. Soon, every lawman and bounty hunter in the entire territory would be on the lookout for him as a wanted killer.

Yet this strange calmness that had settled over him made him even more determined to find his brother's killer and now it seemed the logical place was Calder Wells. Yet, somehow, he had to get off this narrow, barely-visible trail. It would not take Trenton long to figure out this was the only way he could take. Very soon, there would be a posse trailing him and these men knew this country far better than he did.

He remained on the trail for another hour, frequently casting questing glances over his shoulder, searching for any moving shadow that would give away a band of men at his back. Then, a mile further on, the trail abruptly swung away to his right, arrowing towards a range of purple hills in the distance.

To his left, however, less than half a mile away, the moonlight glinted off a wide river and beyond it lay hilly, heavily-wooded country. Making up his mind immediately, he pulled on the reins and turned his mount.

Here, the ground was treacherous, pitted with holes and slashed with narrow crevices. But the stallion was a sure-footed animal, used to keeping up a punishing pace across bad terrain. The river, when he reached it, was wide but shallow, less than a couple of feet deep.

Putting his mount into the smoothly-running water, he turned it downstream and allowed it to move at its own pace through the water. He had gone more than a mile before he swung the animal towards the bank. Here, the trees grew almost to the river's edge.

Pulling the stallion to a halt just inside the first stand of pine, he dismounted. From this vantage point he was just able to make out the rough trail he had left. Minutes passed and still there was no movement out there. Then he spotted the bunch of riders spurring their mounts rapidly, throwing up a cloud of dust behind them.

Waiting tensely, he saw them reach the bend in the trail. With a faint sense of relief, he watched as they swung away towards the east without pausing. Making a smoke, he lit the cigarette and drew the smoke deeply into his lungs. His ruse seemed to have worked. None of those men had reckoned on him heading for the river.

Now he had to make a decision. He could either try to find the trail that would take him west towards Calder Wells, or head back for the place where he had left the wagon train and rejoin them.

He finally decided on the latter. He knew he might be placing everyone with that wagon train in danger from the outlaw band who seemed to be running Yellow Buttes. On the other hand, they might reckon riding with that train would be the last thing he would do, that he would head straight for Calder

Wells. Furthermore, Flap Disforth knew this country, had already taken two trains to California.

He, himself, had no idea where Calders Wells was located. It could take him days to find the right trail and all the time there remained the possibility he would run into that posse.

Using the moon and stars as cardinal points to find his direction, he headed across the hills and just as dawn was brightening towards the east, he emerged at the western end of the trail he had taken the previous evening.

In the brightening daylight, he readily made out the tracks of the wagon train. He doubted if they would have travelled far after he had left them. With the ever-present danger of Cal Forden discovering them on his spread, they would make camp soon after darkness had fallen. It was highly unlikely he would allow them to cross as Casson had.

At the back of his mind he was still unsure why the rancher had done this and the uncertainty worried him. The obvious reason was that Casson had known of his brother's presence in this territory, was also aware that Jim had been killed. He would want some advance warning of any other Federal marshal retracing his brother's trail and might have suspected he was such a lawman.

Yet however logical that seemed, Steve had the nagging feeling there was another, deeper reason for Casson's curious actions. Somewhere at the back of his mind, he felt certain he had the answer.

CHAPTER VI

DEADLY AMBUSH

It was an hour later when Steve caught up with Disforth and the wagon train. They had broken camp a short while before and were strung out in a long line, moving through the lush grassland, keeping up a steady pace.

Clearly there had been no attack from Forden's men during the night and most of them seemed to be in high spirits. Riding alongside Ridgeway's wagon, he came upon Melanie's father seated on the buck-board, holding the reins lightly in his hands. A moment later, the girl came from the back and swung herself easily beside him.

There was a broad smile on her face as she said, 'Thank God you got back safely. One of the men reckons he saw a rider heading after you.'

'Did you find out anythin' about your brother?' Ridgeway asked.

'Only that he left Yellow Buttes and took the trail

to Calder Wells. I guess that's where I'll have to head for next.'

He noticed the expression of concern on the girl's face. 'Do you have to keep going on? If these people did kill your brother, they'll stop at nothing until you're dead too.'

Steve drew his lips into a tight line but before he could reply, Disforth came riding up to him. 'I figured your stay in Yellow Buttes would be longer than this. You run into any trouble?'

'Some. I spoke with an old fella who knew quite a lot. Seems my brother uncovered plenty of evidence to hang both Casson and Forden. He had most of it in a report he'd written but before I could find out any more, some coyote shot the old man through the window of his shack.'

'The same *hombre* who followed you there?'

'Could be,' Steve acquiesced. 'But it means I've probably been framed for his murder. Those men will come lookin' for me and I don't want to bring them down on you. They'll have the so-called law with 'em and they'll claim you're aidin' and harbourin' a wanted killer.'

'Well, I for one, don't believe you're a cold-blooded killer,' Melanie declared vehemently. 'And I think that goes for all the others with this train.'

Beside her, Ridgeway nodded his head in agreement.

However, there was still an expression of grave concern on Disforth's face. Steve could understand the thoughts that were doubtless running through his mind at that moment. The entire wagon train was

81

his responsibility, the lives of everyone riding with it were in his hands.

'The trouble as I see it,' he began, scratching the stubble on his chin, 'is that if they do come lookin' for you here, they'll search every bit of the train and that stallion o' yours would be recognized anywhere.'

Steve thought fast before saying, 'Reckon there's only one thing I can do. That posse from Yellow Buttes will soon discover I've given 'em the slip somewhere along the north trail. My guess is they'll send word to Calder Wells and then ride straight for this wagon train.'

'Seems logical to me,' Disforth commented.

Pointing along the trail, Steve indicated the rugged bluffs that bordered it less than a mile away. 'There should be some place there where I can conceal myself. If they do come and find no sign of me ridin' with you, I doubt if they'll bother you again. They'll figure I've either ridden onto Calder Wells or headed for the border.'

Disforth was still dubious but finally he gave a terse nod. 'I just hope so,' he muttered. 'For all our sakes.'

'Be careful,' Melanie said, looking directly at him. 'I know I've said that before but this time you seem to be in more trouble than ever.'

'I will.' Gigging the stallion forward, he rode swiftly along the line of wagons and then headed for the towering bluffs.

Approaching the wagon train, Sheriff Trenton ordered his men to spread out until they were formed up in a line facing the wagons. Turning to face Yarrow, sitting his mount a few yards away, he rasped, 'You see any sign o' that black stallion this *hombre* was ridin'?'

Yarrow ran his cold keen gaze along the train, then shook his head. 'Don't see it,' he admitted.

Trenton turned his head as Disforth rode up. 'Are you in charge o' this train?' he asked coldly.

'That's right. What's all this about? Far as I know there ain't no law against us crossin' the country. The government has opened up all o' this country to settlers, clear to the California border.'

There was a frosty expression on Trenton's fleshy features as he leaned forward a little, staring across at the other. 'We ain't here for that. Far as I'm concerned, you can go where you like. It'll be up to Cal Forden to say whether you get across his land or not. But there was a murder committed in Yellow Buttes last night. A man was shot down in cold blood and we know who did it. As the law there, I want that killer brought to justice.'

'It certainly wasn't anyone ridin' with this train,' Disforth replied.

'You're lyin', mister.' It was Yarrow who spoke. 'I followed that gunhawk when he slipped away from this train last night, the same man I ran into back east when you were warned against crossin' Ed Casson's land. He put up at the hotel in town.'

'That's right,' Trenton interrupted. 'And Seth here saw him slip out a little after midnight and make his way to Zeb Wheeler's shack. That's where he shot him. He never gave him a chance to get a weapon and defend himself. Zeb's shotgun was placed against the wall when we found him.'

Ridgeway spoke up. 'Then if he's a lowdown killer like you say, why would he come back here? We're all peaceable folk on this train and we don't want a murderer ridin' with us.'

'Maybe so, but it seems you allowed him to ride with you from some place back east.' Trenton raised his arm and called, 'Search all o' these wagons.'

Dismounting, the men moved towards the wagons, ordering everyone to step down. The search was thorough with Trenton and Yarrow riding up and down the long line, making certain that every bit was examined. Once the men were sure there was no one concealed inside the interiors, they moved beneath the wagons, checking every inch.

Finally, they moved back to their mounts, shaking their heads. 'There's nobody else here,' one of the men called. 'It seems they're tellin' the truth.'

Disforth noticed the look of disappointment and defeat on Yarrow's thin features. With an effort, he controlled his anger. 'All right, you can get back on board and drive on. But I still think you're hidin' something. If any of you do come up against this killer, there's a reward for his capture, dead or alive. He can't hide for long.'

Turning to face the man on his left, Trenton snapped, 'I want you to ride to Calder Wells and let Sheriff Jessop know of what's happened.'

He waited until the man had ridden off before whirling on Yarrow. 'We're goin' to have a talk with Ed Casson. He'll want to know that this killer has slipped through the net and is still around someplace.'

Swinging his mount, Yarrow led the men back along the trail, his face set in cold, hard lines. Having lost their quarry during the night he had been sure he would have found him concealed somewhere among those wagons.

Now he had a lot of explaining to do to Casson. Certainly they had succeeded in framing this man for murder and soon every lawman in the territory would have his picture on a wanted poster. But he had no way of telling how much Wheeler had told him and in the meantime, with this stranger still on the loose, he represented a threat to all of them. The sooner he was eliminated, the better.

By the time the wagon train drew level with the bluffs there was no sign of the men who had ridden with the posse. Only a slowly dissipating cloud of yellow dust marked their trail. Riding down from the rocky ledges, Steve caught up with Disforth.

From his vantage point high above the plain he had seen most of what had happened when Trenton and his men had searched the wagons. Somehow, he doubted if they would come looking for him there again.

There was a broad grin on the wagon-master's bluff features as he said, 'They sure have you tagged as a cold-blooded killer, Calladine. Reckon if you hadn't told us exactly how it happened, we might have turned you over to 'em.'

'Thanks for what you did,' Steve said gratefully. 'I won't forget this.'

'What do you intend doin' now?'

'If you've no objections, I'll ride with you until we

get close to Calder Wells. That's where I'll find out what happened to my brother. But there's somethin' you can do for me.'

'If I can, I will.'

'My brother came out here to try to clean up this territory. That's why he took the job of Federal marshal and that's why I'm sure he paid for it with his life. Unless I'm mistaken, this whole territory is on the point of blowing itself apart. Somehow, word o' what's happening here has to be taken to the army at Fort Augusta. Is there any man with the train you could spare to ride out there and tell whoever is in charge that I mean to get all the evidence my brother discovered, that if he rides out here, I'll give him enough to hang those responsible.'

He saw the other hesitate, knew that he was asking a lot. It was more than forty miles to the army post and they might need every gun they had if Forden decided to attack them.

'I'll ask around but I can't guarantee anyone will risk makin' that journey. Nobody here knows anythin' about this territory. It wouldn't be difficult for them to get lost in that wilderness out there.'

'You know this region well enough,' Steve replied. 'You could draw a map for them.'

Disforth was still unconvinced but a moment later he rode along the slow-moving wagons, pausing at each one to speak with the driver. He came back ten minutes later and there was a man walking beside him.

Steve felt a sudden shock of surprise as he recognized Melanie's father. 'Matt Ridgeway says he'll do it,' Disforth said.

Before Steve could make a vehement protest, Ridgeway said calmly, 'My daughter can handle those horses, Calladine. I'll take one of 'em and she'll only have three to manage.'

'But if we're hit by Forden's hired killers, she—'

Ridgeway gave a grim smile. 'I reckon you've seen for yourself that she knows how to handle a gun.'

Judging by the expression on the other's face, Steve knew it would be useless to argue. Instead, he said, 'It won't be easy gettin' there. It'll be forty miles through bad country, outlaw country.'

'I'll take my chances,' Ridgeway said grimly. He walked back to the wagon and eased one of the horses from the traces. Reaching into the back of the wagon, Melanie handed him a rifle and some shells.

By the time he came back, Disforth had drawn a rough map on a piece of paper. Pointing, the wagon-master said tautly, 'Ride north from here until you reach the river and then follow it. You should hit the trail from Calder Wells to Fort Augusta by mornin' if you ride through the night. Stick with that and you can't go wrong.'

Ridgeway thrust the paper into his pocket, then swung away from the train around the side of the buttes, dragging a dust cloud behind him. Soon, he was lost to sight in the distance.

'You reckon he'll make it?' Steve asked, a trace of concern in his voice.

'If he steers well clear o' that helltown, he has a good chance,' Disforth replied. 'Now let's get this train on the move again. I won't feel safe until we're well clear o' this cattle country and through those hills yonder.'

Pushing the tired horses and oxen as quickly as they could, they had covered half a dozen miles before entering more rugged country, the outlying foothills of the hills that straddled their path. Riding ahead of the wagons, searching for the easiest way through the high rocky walls of stone, Steve came upon a wide defile that ran, straight and true, through the narrow range.

At first glance, it looked passable but there was something here that ruffled the small hairs on the back of his neck and sent a warning tingle along his spine. Pausing at the end, he allowed his gaze to rove over the scene, taking in every little detail. The defile was wide enough to allow the passage of a wagon with ease but narrowing his eyes, he noticed something he had missed. He had initially thought it was simply a mass of rocks but then he recognized what it was.

The far exit was blocked by the twisted remains of a burnt-out wagon. His lips tightened into a hard line, but that was the only sign he gave that he had noticed it. Evidently others had travelled this way and had never made it.

He had no doubt there were men up there among the rocks overlooking either side of the defile, men waiting until the train rode in. Once they were all inside, those men would open up on them, knowing there was no way the wagons could be turned to head back.

He rode slowly back to where the others stood waiting. 'Can we get through?' Hap called harshly.

'There's an ambush set up for us yonder,' Steve replied thinly. 'They've blocked the far end and they're just waitin' for us to ride in before they open fire.'

Disforth cast an appraising glance along the range, then shook his head slowly. 'There's no way we can move the train that way in either direction. The terrain is too rough and they'd be on our heels before we'd gone half a mile. Not only that, but we need water. There's sure to be a stream on the other side o' these hills but we could go for days before we come across any if we leave this route.'

'We've just one chance,' Steve said solemnly, 'but it'll take split-second timing and a whole heap o' luck if we're to make it.'

Taking off his hat, the other wiped the sweat from his forehead. 'What's your plan?'

'Right now, those men don't know we suspect their presence. I don't doubt they're professional killers, almost certainly ridin' for this *hombre* Forden. I'm pretty sure they won't give themselves away until the whole o' the train is inside that pass. The far end is blocked in the middle, enough to stop any wagon but not a couple o' men on horseback. How good are you with that lariat?' He pointed to the lasso draped over the other's pommel.

For a moment, Disforth looked surprised at the question. Then he said, 'I reckon I can use it as well as the next man. Why?'

'Good. Then this is what we do. You and me ride into that defile real slow ahead o' the train. Once we're halfway through we both ride hell for leather, lasso that wagon that is blocking the way and drag it out into the open. That'll be the signal for the rest o' the train to do likewise. If we're lucky those gunslingers won't be expectin' it and we can give these folk coverin' fire.'

'Hellfire! That would be sheer suicide. They'll all be shot to pieces.'

'It's goin' to be risky but I reckon it's the only chance we've got. If we act fast, I reckon most o' these wagons will make it. We stand a much better chance of fighting 'em off out there in the open than penned up inside the pass.'

Disforth pondered the idea for several moments. It was clear he didn't like it overmuch but as Steve had pointed out, it was the only choice open to them that stood any chance of success.

Finally, he muttered, 'I'll let everybody know what's happenin'. Tell them to keep their heads down and their weapons ready.'

Steve waited impatiently as the other rode along the line of wagons, speaking to everyone in turn. He knew the dangers inherent in what he had proposed and just how slim the chances were of them all getting through.

Disforth came back ten minutes later, his face grim. 'All right,' he said, speaking through his teeth. 'Let's go. Everyone knows what to expect. I just hope this works.'

They rode slowly, side by side, to the entrance of the defile. As the tall rock ledges closed in around him, Steve felt the muscles of his stomach tighten painfully. There was the unmistakable feel of eyes watching his every move.

Beside him, Disforth deliberately faced straight ahead but his gaze was roving continuously over the boulders and ledges above him, searching for the slightest movement. A deep, clinging silence lay over everything.

Behind them, the first wagons moved forward. Steve could guess at the tensions riding the men and women seated behind the horses and oxen, not knowing when the first bullet would strike, or from which direction it would come. When they were halfway along the pass, he tightened his left hand on the reins, his right hand close to the lasso in front of him.

'Now!' He uttered the single word in a low voice. At the same time, he raked spurs along the stallion's flanks sending it leaping forward. Together, he and Disforth rode hell for leather towards the distant exit. Behind them, he picked out the harsh shouts of those driving the wagons, heard the sudden thunder of racing wheels on the rocky floor.

Swiftly, he pulled the lariat from the pommel, whirling it high above his head. Ten feet from the splintered wreck of the obstructing wagon, he let the lasso go, saw the noose settle over a crooked spear of wood. In almost the same instant, Disforth's rope caught at the far side.

Racing their mounts on either side of the obstacle, they continued on at a frantic run, looping their lariats around the pommels.

For a moment, Steve felt the stallion hesitate in mid-stride as the ropes took the strain. Then the tangled mass broke free of the rocks as they dragged it away to one side. Within seconds, Steve had dropped from the saddle and was running back with the wagon-master at his heels.

Already a savage hammering of gunfire had broken out from among the concealing boulders above the pass. Even though the men handling the racing animals were busy concentrating on racing the wagons as quickly as possible, there was return fire pouring into the ledges.

Dropping down among the mass of boulders on one side, Steve slid the Colts from their holsters. A head showed briefly as a gunman shifted his position to get a better shot at the swift-running wagons. Aiming instinctively, Steve squeezed the trigger twice. The first shot ricocheted off the rock but the second took the gunhawk directly between the eyes.

The man lurched sideways and a second later, his body tumbled down the slope directly under the pounding hoofs of one of the horses. On the other side of the pass, Disforth was firing rapidly at any target that showed itself. Two more men fell sprawling among the boulders.

Then the first of the wagons burst clear of the defile, racing out into the open. Others followed in rapid succession. Still the firing went on. Steve felt the wind of a bullet as it scorched past his cheek. Crouching down, he strove to pick out where the rest of Forden's men were.

By now, the churning wheels of the wagons had thrown up a choking cloud of dust and it was becoming difficult to make out details. However, from the volume of gunshots, he reckoned that most of the bushwhackers were concentrated close to the end of the wide pass.

A wagon came careering towards him and one glance told him the driver had been hit. He glimpsed the ugly stain on the other's shirt, high up on the right shoulder. A second fled before he recognized the preacher he had met the first time the Cherokee had attacked.

The man was obviously in a bad way, struggling to control the wildly racing horses. Almost without thinking, Steve thrust himself to his feet, ignoring his own danger. Thrusting the Colt back into its holster, he steadied himself then leapt for the wagon. His fingers caught the wooden rail and he held on grimly for several seconds before he managed to swing himself up.

The preacher was barely conscious as Steve caught at his arm and thrust him back, grabbing for the reins. Pulling hard on them, he managed to steer the jolting wagon clear of the rocks, the rear wheel missing an outjutting spur by inches. Behind him, Disforth was yelling at the top of his voice, urging the remainder on.

Very soon it became clear that Forden had deployed only a small number of men in the ambush, clearly expecting little trouble. The racketing roar of gunfire dwindled, finally ceasing altogether. Out on the plain, the wagons were scattered in little groups.

Turning his attention to the preacher, Steve saw that the slug had struck obliquely across the other's chest, glancing off the bone. Pulling out his kerchief, he pressed it hard against the wound. Fortunately there was very little bleeding and the slug had passed right through the flesh, exiting just beneath his right arm.

'We'll take a look at that once we get the wagons into some kind of order,' Steve said quietly. 'You were lucky. Not much more than a scratch.'

'What about the others?' muttered the preacher, running his tongue around his dry lips.

'I reckon we got off pretty lightly,' Steve replied. 'Forden either reckoned nothin' could go wrong and sent only a handful o' men, or he intends usin' the rest of his force for some other purpose.'

'To attack us again?'

'Somehow, I doubt that. From what I've learned there's been bad blood between Casson and Forden for a long time. Sooner or later, one of 'em is goin' to try to take over the whole o' this territory. I just hope Ridgeway gets word to the army in time or there's goin' to be a full-scale range war here. Unless we can reach those mountains yonder, we'll find ourselves in the middle of it.'

CHAPTER VII

FUGITIVE

The wagon train was little more than a dot, shrouded in dust, when Steve pulled off the trail and headed north towards Calder Wells. From what Disforth had told him, the town lay close to the tall hills he could just make out in the distance.

For the past three days, the wagons had struggled westward, expecting another attack at any moment, but strangely, it had never materialized. Whatever game Cal Forden was playing, it seemed he had temporarily forgotten about them.

Even though the sun was now westering, the heat still lay in the shimmering air. All around him, dust devils danced in the whirling eddies of wind that gusted across this hostile land. Here, in the malpais, there were no tracks to follow, nothing to even indicate that others had ever passed this way. Any that might have been made in the past had been obliterated by the shifting dust that covered everything. Only the hills now provided him with a quartering point on which to fix his direction.

More than once, he had to knock the dust from his shirt before it got through to his skin. Even rubbing it abraded his flesh as it mixed with the sweat on his body.

He drank the water from his canteen sparingly, knowing it would probably be noon the next day before he sighted the town and there was little chance of finding a waterhole in this infernal desert-land.

Taking his time, he allowed the stallion to pick its own pace here. In places, its hoofs sank deeply into the unstable ground, throwing the animal temporarily off balance but it quickly righted itself, somehow sensing where the most treacherous stretches of the malpais lay.

As he rode, his thoughts drifted and swirled in his mind. Maybe Disforth and the others were right, maybe he was riding through this blistering hell on a fool's errand with no chance of ever finding out whether his brother had been killed and, if so, the identity of his killer.

In addition, strangers riding into a helltown like Calder Wells was reputed to be were looked upon with suspicion. If he was to start asking questions of the wrong people, he could find every gun against him.

With his shadow growing perceptibly longer to his right, he focused his attention on the distant hills. Up ahead, the ground became even rougher with gaunt, sky-rearing buttes clawing from the ground, all etched into fantastic shapes by endless ages of abrasion and the scouring wind.

Half an hour later, the terrain worsened. Deep, razor-edged crevices slashed the ground in all directions, slowing his mount even further as he was forced to detour around them. By the time the sun touched the horizon in a glaring crimson glow, he was deep within a rocky defile, its upper reaches glowing redly in the last vestiges of sunlight.

Here, the wind had increased in ferocity as it funnelled between the rock walls. Whistling eerily among the numerous clefts and gullies, it shrieked in his ears. Now, he rode low in the saddle, his hat-brim pulled down to just above his eyes, his keen gaze searching for a place where he might rest up for the night.

For several hundred yards, he saw no place where he could pull off the ravine bottom into a spot of relative comfort and escape from the wind. The rock-face seemed to extend endlessly in solid walls along either side.

Not until he was approaching the far end of the narrow passage through the rocks did he notice a wide shelf that jutted out like a stone tongue from the scattered boulders to his left. Wearily, he turned the stallion towards it, sliding from the saddle.

The jerked beef from his saddlebag was tough and he chewed on it several times before washing it down with water. So far, he had seen no sign of life since leaving the wagon train. Not even a lizard or scorpion had disturbed the emptiness of the land through which he had ridden. It was as if this was the one place on Earth that God had forgotten, leaving it as it had existed for millions of years.

Once he had finished eating and the darkness had come down with only the faint starlight and a wan glow from the thin yellow sickle of the moon low in the heavens to give him any light, he got up and walked to the edge of the shelf. There was no sound beyond the small noises of the stallion moving around.

Shivering a little in the cold night air, he stood there for a full ten minutes, straining his vision to pick out any movement, not relaxing his vigilance for a single second. Out here, in the wilderness, appearances could be deceptive.

Men sometimes roamed these deserted spaces, men wanted in half a dozen states, trying to stay one jump ahead of the law. At a rough estimate, he reckoned he was still some twenty miles from Calder Wells.

Lighting a cigarette, he pulled the sweet-smelling smoke into his lungs. It brought a little warmth back into his body. After the scorching heat of the day, with the temperature dropping rapidly at nightfall, a man felt the chill more than normal.

The moon lifted slowly in the east, throwing its light into the defile, picking out everything in a stark monochrome. Finishing the smoke, he took out his blanket and rolled himself into it, stretching out on the smooth rock.

He deliberately placed one of the Colts beside him where he could reach it in an instant. Out here, in the badlands, he didn't expect any trouble but a man stayed alive only by taking no chances.

When he woke it was still dark, but there was a

faint flush of brightness towards the east. For a moment he lay quite still, his hand around the Colt, finger on the trigger. Every sense was alert as he searched around for whatever had woken him so abruptly.

Then the sound reached him again, that of a fast-running horse. A moment later, a couple of shots rang out in rapid succession. He was on his feet in an instant, easing himself into the utter darkness of the nearby rocks.

The rider must have stopped for the sound of hoofbeats immediately died away and he picked out a low, moaning cry. Seconds later, there was the unmistakable beat of more riders approaching swiftly.

Moving forward an inch at a time, Steve moved around outjutting spurs of rock, finally coming up against a line of boulders. Immediately beyond them lay more open ground. Peering intently through a narrow crack, he instantly made out the two riders spurring their mounts towards where he crouched.

Lifting his head cautiously, he glanced down towards the ground directly below him. A horse lay on its side, unmoving. Evidently it had been shot by one of the approaching men. Nearer at hand lay a huddled figure, almost invisible in the dimness.

Unaware of his presence, the two riders reined their mounts, dropping swiftly from the saddle.

'You reckon you could run out on us, Collins,' rasped one of the men, levelling his Colt on the prone figure.

'Guess we should put a slug in him and get it over

with,' muttered the second man hoarsely. 'Ain't no sense takin' him back into town.'

'Why not? It'd give me great pleasure to see him swing.'

There was a pause and then the second man said, 'Sure. But he's got no mount now and I sure don't aim to carry him back over my saddle.'

'Then we shoot him, but first, he's goin' to get the whippin' he deserves. When I'm finished with him, he'll be beggin' us to kill him.'

Before he had finished speaking, the man had taken a long bullwhip from his saddle. He flicked it through the air a couple of times, then brought it down hard on the man lying in front of him.

A faint moan of agony escaped the fallen man's lips as the lash bit deeply into his flesh. Grinning viciously, the other lifted the whip for a second time, then froze, his hand in midair, as Steve rose up from behind the rocks.

'Try that again and I'll drill you,' he said with a deceptive calmness.

Both men stared up, stunned surprise visible on their bearded features.

'What the hell?' snarled the first man thickly.

'You heard what I said. Drop that whip and those guns.'

He saw the men hesitate for a moment. Then the man with the whip dropped it at his feet. As if it had been a signal, both men lifted their guns to line them up on Steve.

Before they could use them, Steve's Colt spat flame twice. Eyes staring in mute astonishment, both men staggered as the slugs tore into them. Then, almost as one, they slumped onto the rocks and lay still. Cautiously, Steve edged down the treacherous slope to where the dark figure lay propped against a boulder.

White eyes staring up at him, lips drawn back in pain, the other said hoarsely, 'Thanks, mistuh. Those two meant to kill me.'

'You runnin' from your boss?' Steve asked, holstering the Colt.

'Runnin' from Calder Wells. They was goin' to hang me there at sun-up.'

Squatting down beside him, Steve examined the ugly weal on the other's chest.

'Just lie there and I'll get some water. Then I'll clean that up for you.'

He came back a couple of minutes later with his canteen and offered it to the other. The man drank sparingly before handing the canteen back.

'Thanks again, mistuh. Guess you saved my life. Ain't many who'd do that fer the likes o' me.'

'I don't like to see anyone get an uneven chance,' Steve replied tautly. 'Why were they goin' to hang you. Caught you stealin'?'

The other shook his head. 'I was just a swamper at the hotel. I ain't never stole anythin' in my life.'

After cleaning the flesh where the weal had bled, Steve sat back on his haunches. He knew this was not an uncommon occurrence. Black slaves sometimes tried to escape from their masters and were inevitably killed without question if they were caught.

But deep inside, something told him there was

more to this. Slaves performing menial work were usually tolerated, even in places like Calder Wells. Life might be hard for them but they were fed and given a place to live. So why had this man tried to run away and, more to the point, why were those men after him?

Before he could speak, however, the other said, 'What's your name, mistuh? You don't look like those two yonder.' He inclined his head towards the two bodies sprawled on the rocks.

'Calladine,' Steve said shortly.

He noticed the brief gust of expression that flashed across the other's features at the mention of his name.

Gripping the man's arm, he said tautly, 'You've heard that name before, haven't you?'

The other made no answer for almost a minute and Steve was on the point of repeating the question, more insistently this time, when the other said slowly, 'He was your brother, wasn't he?'

'Are you talkin' about Jim Calladine?' Steve's voice was as taut as an iron bar. 'You know what happened to him.'

Reaching for the canteen, the other took another swallow, then said, 'I know, Mistuh Calladine. That's why I was runnin' from Calder Wells, why those two men were trailin' me, to stop me from tellin'; tellin' everything I know.'

'He's dead, ain't he?'

Nodding slowly, the other replied, 'Yessir, he's dead.'

'And you know who shot him?'

102

There was a long pause as if the other was unsure how to answer the question. Then, 'He weren't shot. No, sir. He was knifed in the back.'

Mechanically, Steve replaced the cap on the canteen, struggling to absorb this information, to make sense of it.

Finally, he asked, 'You saw it happen? You know who killed him?'

'It was a while back, late at night. I was jest sweepin' out and I saw your brother comin' out of the saloon. Guess he'd made a lot of enemies in town, pryin' into Cal Forden's affairs.'

'Cal Forden?' Steve recalled the name.

'A big man in Calder Wells. He owns most o' that town.' A brief hiatus, then the other went on, 'This man follered your brother along the street. I saw them talkin', seemed to be arguin' between themselves. Then your brother walked away and that was when he was knifed.'

'Give me the name of the man who did it,' Steve demanded harshly.

With a stiff movement, the other got to his feet. 'If you're figurin' on goin' after him, ferget it, Mistuh Calladine. I know how you feel but this *hombre* is a killer. Ain't ever seen him carry a gun but he's like lightnin' with a knife. I seen him skewer a man through the heart afore he had a chance to draw his gun.'

'His name,' Steve persisted.

'Don't know his real name. Ain't ever heard it. Folk jest call him Lobo.'

'Thanks for the information,' Steve said thinly.

'So what are yuh goin' to do?'

A grim smile twitched Steve's lips. 'Guess I'm goin' to ride on into Calder Wells, find this *hombre* Lobo, and kill him.'

'You'll be a dead man if yuh do.'

'Mebbe so, mebbe not. And I'm takin' you back with me.'

A spasm of pure terror crossed the other's features and he started back as if he had been struck in the face. 'Yuh saved me from those killers, yuh ain't takin' me back. They'll string me up as soon as I show my face in that town.'

'I need you to point out this Lobo. If I was to ask about him either someone will warn him, or he'll have a band o' killers waiting for me in the shadows.'

Steve saw the other hesitate, knew that fear was still the dominant emotion in his mind, but there was now something else, some resolve that was stiffening him. Finally, he straightened, squaring his shoulders. 'Yuh saved my life, Mistuh Calladine. Guess I owe you that.' Pausing momentarily, he went on, 'Will yuh give me a gun?'

Turning, Steve pointed to the two dead gunmen lying nearby. 'Take one o' theirs. They won't be needing 'em where they've gone. You can take one o' their horses.'

By now, the dawn had brightened and there was a red flush touching the underside of a long bar of cloud. Leading the other back to the draw, they ate a cold meal, squatting on the broad shelf. Now Steve could see his companion clearly. He judged him to be around forty but the grey-white hair made him

104

look appreciably older.

'Guess I don't know your name.' he said, glancing across at the other.

'They call me Jefferson Collins.' There was a faint trace of pride in the man's voice. 'My mammy named me after the President.'

'It's a good name,' Steve commented. 'Well, Jefferson, once I've dealt with this snake Lobo, we get out o' town fast.'

The other nodded in vehement agreement.

Going on, Steve added, 'Once we're clear, we head west.'

'West?'

'That's right. I came here with a wagon train from Clinton. They went on yesterday afternoon. If we're lucky we should catch up with 'em in two or three days and we'll be safe there.'

Fifteen minutes later, they climbed into the saddle. The heavy gunbelt his companion had buckled about his waist seemed oddly out of place and for a moment, Steve wondered whether the other would be able to use those guns if anything went wrong.

As they rode out, Steve asked, 'I reckon you must know a lot about this town, Jefferson. Any place where a couple o' men could hole up?'

His companion pondered that for a while, then shook his head. 'Won't be easy findin' any place. Forden has men everywhere and he don't like men wanderin' around town that he knows nothin' about.'

He paused for a moment as a fresh thought occurred to him. 'There might be one place.'

'Where's that?'

'There's the old assay office right near the far edge o' town. There used to be gold in them hills yonder but that were more'n twenty years ago. The office ain't been used for nigh on fifteen years. It's all locked up now since that strike petered out.'

'Then I guess that's where we make for.'

'Won't be easy in daylight,' warned the other. 'Too many folk on the streets. Any stranger would be noticed at once and I guess they all know my face.'

'You reckon we should wait until nightfall?'

Jefferson gave an almost imperceptible nod. He still seemed uneasy at the prospect of returning to Calder Wells.

'Guess you're right.' When he had left the main trail, Steve had intended riding into Calder Wells as soon as he got there. But then he had been alone, meaning to make discreet enquiries about his brother.

Now he had all the information he needed and it was no longer necessary for him to risk asking around. There was also Jefferson's presence to be taken into consideration. A man riding into town like this in the company of an armed slave, would almost certainly be on the receiving end of a bullet.

They rode on for a couple of hours with the heat-head rising all around them. By now, the hills were less than ten miles away, forming a massive barrier along the horizon.

Jefferson reined up his mount abruptly and sat wiping the sweat from his eyes. Then he pointed. 'There's the trail into Calder Wells, Mistuh

Calladine. Reckon we'd better get under cover. Plenty o' riders use that trail durin' the daytime.'

Steve turned to ask the obvious question – where was there any cover from this pitiless sun? But already his companion had pulled hard on the reins and was making for an immense butte, a gigantic formation of red rock. Around its base lay tumbled masses of stones far higher than a man on horseback.

Following Collins, he saw that here the ground dipped sharply, forming a deep natural basin. Even though the sun was not far from its zenith, the whole area lay in the shadow of the butte. Once inside the depression, they dismounted and hobbled their mounts.

Now he was no longer in the savage glare of sunlight, Steve felt the nagging ache behind his temples beginning to ease. He sat with his back against the rough rock, his legs thrust out straight in front of him.

A few feet away, Jefferson sat, eyes staring at nothing. It was impossible to guess at the thoughts passing through his mind.

Building a smoke, Steve lit it and inhaled deeply. 'Tell me what you know about my brother,' he said after a long silence. 'Did you know him well?'

'Guess nobody knew much about him,' replied the other slowly. 'I had him figgered for a lawman when he first rode in and put up at the hotel. He didn't wear no star but some o' the Federal marshals work in secret and havin' no star didn't mean a thing. But when he asked me if I knew Cal Forden, I then had him figgered for some drifter lookin' for a job.'

'Did he ever work for this man, Forden?'

'No, sir. Didn't work for anybody. Leastways not as far as I know.'

'So how come he was killed by this *hombre*, Lobo?'

'Lobo works for Forden. Fact is, he's Forden's right-hand man on the ranch. Like I said, he never carries a gun. That's what makes him so dangerous. He's fast and can throw these knives fifty feet, and they always find their mark. Any stranger who called him out would be dead on his feet with a knife in his heart before he could clear leather.'

'But you said my brother got a knife in the back, that he never had a chance to draw.'

'That's sure how it happened. Lobo jest pulled a knife and got him in the back.'

Tossing the cigarette-butt onto the rock, Steve ground it out under his heel. 'And you saw this happen? That's why those men were after you, to stop you talkin'.'

'That's the God's truth, Mistuh Calladine.'

Frowning, Steve pulled the Colts from their holsters and refilled the empty chambers. 'I believe you,' he remarked thinly.

Daylight was almost completely gone when they stirred themselves. Even in the shade thrown by the massive butte, the afternoon had been scorchingly hot and now they had very little water left.

Tightening the cinch under his mount's belly, he climbed slowly into the saddle. Beside him, Jefferson did likewise, his broad features inscrutable. Eyeing the other closely, Steve said, 'I've been thinkin', Jefferson. It's asking a mighty lot o' you, going back into that helltown just to point out this killer. If you—'

The other shook his head vehemently. 'Yuh saved my life back there, Mistuh Calladine. If yuh hadn't come along when yuh did, I'd be danglin' from a rope by now. I'm with yuh all the way.'

'You sure you know how to handle those guns?' Steve doubted if the other had ever fired a gun in his life.

'I ain't no gunman but if I got to, I'll use 'em. Yuh can count on that.'

'Good, then let's go. We'll circle the town and come to that assay office from the rear. That way, we have a chance of gettin' there without bein' seen.'

Quietly, they moved out of the basin. Underfoot, the treacherous shifting sand made the footing difficult for the horses but finally they reached the rim. In the distance, the lights of Calder Wells were just visible where the town huddled against the hills.

Now Steve was content to follow his companion. It was soon evident that the other knew the layout of the town like the back of his hand. As they came within earshot, noise and music spilled out in a cacophony of noise. There seemed to be a lot of activity going on and occasionally, a shot would ring out above the background din.

From the direction of most of the noise, Steve estimated that much of the population of Calder Wells was gathered in the various saloons. There would be some on the streets but around the periphery of the town there was no one in sight.

Without speaking, Jefferson circled a short row of wooden buildings and crossed a stretch of open ground. Here, he signalled Steve to halt his mount. Tethering them within a small stand of windbent trees, they went forward on foot towards the small wooden building Jefferson indicated. Moments later, they were pressed hard against the rear wall.

Here there was a single square window. There was no glass in it but two fairly stout metal bars had been placed there to protect any gold that had been deposited there during the time of the strike twenty years earlier.

Feeling around it, Steve soon found that the intervening years had weakened the once-sturdy frame. Taking out his knife, he worked the blade around the edges. Within a couple of minutes it came free and he withdrew it carefully, making no sound.

One after the other, they squeezed their way inside. Standing quite still until his eyes became accustomed to the pitch blackness, Steve just managed to make out a small table in the middle and a large safe standing against one wall. There was a door at the far end and going through they found themselves in the small front office.

The dusty window looked directly onto the main street outside. Motioning his companion to stay behind him, he edged slowly towards the window, pressing himself hard against the wall.

From there he was able to see a sizeable length of the street and across it to where two saloons stood side by side. Several horses were tethered to the hitching rails that fronted them and there were at least a couple of dozen men standing on the far boardwalk.

Heavy footsteps immediately outside caused him to draw back quickly. Shadows passed across the window and there was the sound of harsh voices. Slowly, the sounds receded and Steve allowed his pent-up breath to go in a long exhalation.

Beside him, Jefferson was on his knees near the window. Cautiously, he raised his head, staring across the street towards the saloons.

'You see any sign o' this Lobo?' Steve asked in a low, hushed whisper.

Jefferson shook his head. 'He's not among those men there. Could be he's inside one o' the saloons.'

'Keep your eyes open but be careful you ain't seen.'

Easing back into the dark shadows, Steve waited. He was a patient man. He had come a long way for this moment. A little more time would make no difference.

Several more men walked past the office but each time Jefferson's sharp ears caught the sound of their approach and he ducked down, out of sight.

After a full ten minutes of watching, Jefferson said in a barely audible whisper, 'Could be Lobo ain't in town tonight. He may be out on Forden's spread or at the ranch.'

He broke off sharply at the sound of riders approaching from the far end of the street. A small band of men rode by on the other side, reining up in front of the nearer saloon. Steve heard his companion's sharp intake of breath a moment later and moved stealthily forward.

'That's him, Mistuh Calladine. That's Lobo, the

man who murdered your brother. The one jest steppin' down from the saddle yonder.'

Over Jefferson's bowed head, Steve made out the man just moving up onto the opposite boardwalk. In the light spilling through the saloon windows it was easy to make out his features.

Thin, almost to the point of gauntness, the other had close-set eyes and a thin pencil moustache. His gimlet mouth was pressed into a hard, tight line. Jet-black curly hair showed just beneath his hat.

'You're sure that's the man?'

'Yessir. I never ferget a face. He's the one.'

Steve kept his gaze fixed on Lobo until he had disappeared inside the saloon, then glanced down at his companion.

'Now here's what I want you to do. Go back to where we left the horses and wait there for me. If I don't show up in half an hour, saddle up and ride west for that wagon train. Tell them Steve Calladine sent you. Got that?'

'Yessir, I got that. But you ain't goin' into that saloon after him, are yuh? They'll kill yuh for sure.'

Steve smiled grimly in the darkness. 'If they do, I'll sure as hell take a few o' them with me and Lobo will be the first.'

CHAPTER VIII

SWIFT
RETRIBUTION

Once Jefferson had slipped away into the shadows at the rear of the assay office, Steve made his way along the narrow alley that bordered it until he came out into the main street. There had been three men riding with Lobo when he had come into town. How many would back the killer's play, he didn't know.

Drawing in a deep breath, he eased the Colts in their holsters and then stepped across the dusty street and pushed open the saloon doors. Hesitating for only an instant, he swung his gaze around the place. It looked no different to a hundred other saloons along the frontier.

The bar ran three quarters of the way along the far wall. The remaining space there was occupied by a small stage. A little man wearing a bowler hat sat at a piano, running his hands idly over the keys. It was clear that very few of the customers were taking any notice of him.

Steve picked out Lobo almost at once, seated at a table in the far corner, his back to the wall. The three men who had entered with him were seated around it. One of them had produced a pack of cards and was dealing them to the others.

Giving them only a cursory glance, Steve stepped up to the bar. The bartender, standing only a few feet away, deliberately took his time sidling over. When he stood facing Steve, he said softly, 'You're a stranger in Calder Wells, mister. Hope you're not in town lookin' for trouble.'

Steve grinned. 'I never go lookin' for trouble, friend. But if it starts, I sure as hell finish it.' Drawing the bottle and glass towards him, he added, 'You seem a mite nervous when someone rides in. Any reason for it?'

Saying nothing, the other stepped back a little way, his glance dropping towards the back of the bar.

Straightening up, Steve poured some of the whiskey into the glass. Lifting it to his lips, he stared at the bartender over the rim. 'Don't even think o' makin' a play for that shotgun you've got stashed there. It's likely to be the last thing you do.'

After a brief pause, the other said quietly, his tone belying the look of fear in his narrowed eyes, 'Guess we like to know who rides in here, and why.'

'That's not a very friendly attitude.' Steve poured more of the whiskey into the glass and sipped it slowly, aware that several of the men in the room were eyeing him closely.

One of them abruptly scraped back his chair and

stood up. He was a big man, broad, but not with fat. There was several days' growth of beard on his swarthy features.

'Where are you from, mister?' There was a sneering note in the other's coarse voice.

'A lot o' places,' Steve replied calmly. 'Which one would you be interested in?'

For a moment, the other was at a loss for words at this reply. Then his eyes narrowed. He let his glance drop towards the Colts at Steve's waist. 'I'd say you're some kinda lawman. We got ourselves a sheriff here and we don't take too kindly to others movin' in.'

'I'm no lawman and I've got no quarrel with you.' As he spoke Steve stepped away from the counter. The man was clearly looking for trouble, ready for anything.

Over in the far corner, Lobo was apparently concentrating solely on the card game but Steve knew he was watching everything closely.

Deliberately, not once taking his glance from the big man's face, Steve advanced on him. The other's right hand hovered close to the gun at his hip and his thick lips were twisted into a sneering grin.

'That's far enough, mister,' growled the other. 'Make your play if you've a mind to but—'

Before the man could finish speaking, Steve had side-stepped. His left fist came round in a haymaker that caught the other flush on the chin. His head went back as the blow connected. Steve saw his eyes roll up in his head. Without uttering a sound, he went back, his head striking the side of the table. One glance was enough to tell Steve the man was out cold.

'Anyone else want to make trouble?' Steve asked.

When no one answered, he moved back to the bar, leaning his elbows nonchalantly on the counter, eyeing every man in turn.

After a pause, one of the men said, 'Reckon Jake spoke outta turn, mister. But men have ridden here to make trouble and—'

'What kind o' trouble did my brother make when he rode in some time ago?' Steve let the question hang in the air like a threat.

'Your brother?' queried another man.

'I guess Lobo knows what I'm talkin' about. Jim Calladine, the man he knifed in the back without givin' him a chance to defend himself.' There was a sudden crash as the table in the corner went over, cards scattering in all directions.

With an oath, Lobo pulled himself smoothly to his feet. 'So you're that low-life's brother. Somehow, I figgered you'd show up sometime. What took you so long? Maybe you're as yeller as your brother.'

With an effort, Steve thrust his anger down. He knew the other was deliberately trying to rile him, to force him into doing something foolish. 'Just keep on talkin', Lobo. You ain't going to talk your way out of here alive and if any o' your friends are thinking of buttin' in, they'll go the same way.'

Very slowly, Lobo walked around the side of the upturned table, motioning to the other three to remain where they were.

When he was some ten feet away, he stopped, poised on his feet like a cat. Running a finger over his moustache, he said, 'So you reckon you're fast

116

with those guns.' He drew his coat aside. 'As you can see, I don't carry a gun so if you want to shoot down an unarmed man, then go ahead, but—'

His flow of words was merely a ruse, an attempt to catch Steve off guard. But the other was ready for him. Lobo's hand flashed down for the long-bladed knife in his belt.

Even as he raised his arm, the Colt in Steve's hand spat gunflame. For a long moment, Lobo stood there, eyes wide with shock and stunned surprise. Then the knife fell from his fingers and he went over backward, falling across the unconscious man Steve had hit earlier.

Before anyone could move, Steve swung the Colt in a wide arc, covering everyone in the room. 'Everybody stay right where they are and keep their hands where I can see 'em,' he said in a low, deadly voice.

Very slowly, he backed towards the doors. Reaching them, he thrust back with his shoulders, stepping out onto the boardwalk, then stopped as a gunbarrel was pushed hard into his back.

A voice grated, 'Hold it right there, stranger. Drop that gun.'

Reluctantly, cursing himself for not realizing there might also be danger outside, Steve allowed the gun to fall to the ground.

'That's better,' continued the voice. 'Now turn around and step down into the street.'

Steve turned. The man standing there was short and stocky. There was a star on his shirt and the gun in his hand was rock steady, levelled at his chest.

Before Steve could speak, several men pushed their way out of the saloon. 'He just shot Lobo, Sheriff,' called one of them. 'Gunned him down in cold blood.'

'I shot him when he tried to kill me with that knife of his,' Steve muttered. 'He knifed my brother in the back, right here in Calder Wells.'

'Cal Forden ain't goin' to like this when he gets word of it,' said another man. 'Lobo was his best man.'

'And once Lobo's brother hears of it, there'll be hell to pay,' the first man butted in. 'Best we string this *hombre* up right now and save ourselves a heap o' trouble.'

'We wait until I hear what Mister Forden has to say,' the sheriff said harshly. He peered closely at Steve. 'Besides, this *hombre* could be the same coyote who shot that man in Yellow Buttes. The description I got yesterday sure fits him.'

'So what are you goin' to do with him, Jessop?'

'He'll be quite safe in one o' the cells for the night,' Jessop replied tersely. 'One o' you men ride out to Forden's place and tell him what's happened. There'll be plenty o' time to hang him in the morning.'

Still grumbling, the men backed off. One of them drew himself into the saddle of a nearby horse. 'Just make sure he's still here when I get back with Forden, Sheriff,' he called sharply. 'Otherwise he'll take this whole town apart. And while you're about it, I suggest you send word to Seth Yarrow. Guess he has a right to know his brother has been killed by this *hombre*.'

'He'll be here,' Jessop replied. 'Now the rest of you get back to your drinkin' and leave him to me.'

Some of the men seemed on the point of arguing further but after a moment they all drifted back inside the saloon.

Still keeping the Colt on him, the sheriff bent and picked up Steve's gun and thrust it into his belt. 'Now git,' he said, prodding Steve in the back.

Knowing it would be useless to try anything, Steve crossed the street where he was pushed through the doors of the sheriff's office. The news that Yarrow was Lobo's brother had shaken him.

There was no doubt that Yarrow had known his brother had murdered Jim. In a bizarre way that explained why the other had framed him for Wheeler's death.

'Now unbuckle that gunbelt and place it on the desk,' Jessop said. 'Don't make any funny moves or I'll plug you where you stand.'

Slowly, Steve did as he was told, knowing the other meant every word he said.

'I don't suppose it's any good tellin' you what really happened,' he said.

'Nope. I've heard all I want to hear. And if you are this killer from Yellow Buttes, I reckon hangin' is too good for you.'

Taking down a bunch of keys from the wall, the other ushered him along a short passage at the rear, opening one of the cell doors and motioning Steve inside. The door closed with a harsh, metallic sound and the key was turned in the lock.

'You're makin' a big mistake, Sheriff. I killed

nobody in Yellow Buttes,' he said, staring at the other through the bars. 'My brother was murdered by that *hombre*, Reckon I've got the right to avenge his killin'.'

'Sure you have – if that was how it was. Only those men in there all claim you shot him down without a chance.'

'They would say that. All friends of his, probably all scared o' this man, Forden. Fine town you run here, Sheriff, where a man gets hanged on the say-so of a bunch of gunslingers.'

'Count yourself lucky you got tonight,' Jessop grated surlily. 'If those men had their way, you'd be stretchin' rope by now.'

A moment later, the lawman moved away, leaving Steve in total darkness. Carefully, he felt his way around. A few moments later, he knew the inside of the cell as surely as if he could see everything in broad daylight.

There was an iron bed placed against one side wall with a couple of blankets thrown over it. The opposite wall was bare. At the rear was a small square window that looked out onto the night sky. Three iron bars were set across it.

He tested them carefully, wrapping his fingers around them and pulling with all his strength. They refused to budge. Quite clearly, there was no escape that way.

In the distance, he could still hear the sound of drunken voices singing bawdy songs in the saloons. By now, he guessed, they would have taken Lobo's body to the morgue. Briefly, he wondered how long it would be before this man Forden arrived in town.

It was already clear that he was the real law in Calder Wells. Whatever he said was carried out without question. The sheriff merely obeyed any orders he was given.

After pacing the cell a couple of times he sat down on the edge of the bed, staring into the darkness. He had never felt so helpless in his entire life, and all for one stupid mistake. He should have realized that the sound of the shot might bring someone running to the saloon.

Or was shooting such a commonplace occurrence in this helltown that normally no one would have paid any attention. Maybe it was just unfortunate that the sheriff happened to be there at that particular moment.

Stretching out on the uncomfortable bed, he clasped his hands behind his neck. What was Jefferson doing now, he wondered. He felt sure the other would do exactly as he had told him. Once he failed to show up, Jefferson would fork his mount and head west, hoping to catch up with that wagon train before anyone in town caught up with him again.

After an hour or so, the noise in the street diminished. There came the unmistakable sounds of riders departing.

Going over to the cell door, he peered along the passage. There was a thin strip of yellow light showing a few feet away and he guessed that Jessop was still there in the office, would probably remain there all night, or at least until Forden showed up.

Another ten minutes passed and then he picked out the sound of the street door opening and someone came in. Sharp voices sounded and then there was a dull crash as if something heavy had fallen.

Tensing himself against the wall, Steve waited. His only thought was that Forden had arrived in a foul mood, intent on taking him out and hanging him from the nearest convenient tree.

The door at the end of the passage swung open and a dark figure stood there, silhouetted against the pale yellow glow.

'Yuh in there, Mistuh Calladine?' Jefferson's low voice echoed along the passage.

'Over here,' he called softly.

A moment later, Jefferson was standing outside the cell, the bunch of keys in one hand. Quickly, he tried one in the lock, then another. The third opened the door and Steve slipped out beside him.

'We got to hurry,' Jefferson murmured. 'There are men still around on the streets.'

Going into the office, Steve buckled on his gunbelt. Jessop lay limply over the desk, his head to one side. He was evidently out cold.

'How the hell did you find me?' Steve whispered. 'I told you to stay with the horses and then take off if I didn't show up.'

The other's teeth showed in a wide grin. 'I figgered the safest place for me was back in the assay office,' he replied. 'I saw what happened when you backed out o' the saloon and guessed you'd killed the man who murdered your brother. When I saw the sheriff bring you here, I waited until things quietened down a little.'

While he had been speaking, he had moved to the street door, opening it a little way and peering out. He waited for a few moments and then signalled Steve forward.

'Hold it for a minute,' Steve muttered. 'There's somethin' else I've got to do before we leave here.'

Jefferson turned an anxious face in his direction. 'Ain't nothin' else yuh can do here now that Lobo's dead. We've got to get away afore Forden rides in.'

Steve gripped the other's arm tightly. 'Who's the lawyer in this godforsaken town?'

'Hal Simpson. But what do you want with him?'

'I'm thinkin' he might have somethin' I need,' Steve replied grimly. 'Can you get me to him without bein' seen?'

For a moment, Steve thought the other was going to protest, but all he said was, 'Yuh sure don't make things easy for yourself, Mistuh Calladine.'

Together, they slipped into the dark alley, cutting away from the main street. Silently, Jefferson led the way along the backs of the saloons and stores that lined that side of the street. Then they had entered a small, paved yard. In front of them was the rear of a squat, two-storey building.

Pointing, Jefferson said in a low whisper, 'This is where Mistuh Simpson lives. If he ain't in one o' the saloons, this is where he'll be.'

Blinking his eyes to accustom them to the dark shadows here, Steve padded towards one of the windows. Taking out his knife, he carefully inserted the blade and a moment later, the catch slid aside.

The window was stiff and for an instant, he thought it was jammed through lack of use.

Then it slid up with a scraping of warped wood. Swiftly, he eased himself inside. Turning to where Jefferson stood, he murmured, 'Stay here and keep your eyes open for any trouble.'

The room was evidently the kitchen and in almost total darkness except where a thin strip of yellow light showed beneath the far door. Obviously, the lawyer was at home. Hefting the Colt in his right hand, Steve turned the door handle slowly, opening it a little way.

Simpson was seated at a long desk, his back to him. There was a sheaf of papers in front of him. Advancing into the room, Steve levelled the gun on the lawyer. Some strange instinct must have warned the man of danger for he turned abruptly in the swivel chair, one hand going towards a drawer.

'Don't try to go for the gun you've got stashed there,' Steve said harshly. 'You'll be dead before you can reach it.'

Reluctantly, the other withdrew his hand and stared unbelievingly at Steve. 'Who the hell are you?' he rasped thinly. 'And what are you doin' here, breakin' into my house and pullin' a gun on me?'

Steve smiled thinly as he walked forward and stood directly beside the other. 'I reckon you know who I am. Jim Calladine's brother.'

A sudden gust of recognition and fear flashed across the lawyer's features. 'Then you're that killer Sheriff Jessop got word about. I heard that you'd shot down Lobo in the saloon. I don't know how you got

124

out o' jail, but you won't leave this town alive.'

'Then I've got nothin' to lose, have I? Either you tell me what I want to know, or I'll kill you just as I killed that snake Lobo.'

Now there was real fear in the other's eyes. He squirmed nervously in his chair, his gaze riveted on the gun in Steve's hand. 'There ain't anythin' I can tell you.'

'No?' With a sudden movement, Steve rammed the gunbarrel hard into the other's chest. 'If you want to live, you're goin' to open that safe yonder. I reckon you've got enough evidence locked away in there to indict both Casson and Forden for murder, runnin' guns to the Indians and a host of other crimes.'

Reaching down, he caught the other's arm and hauled him roughly to his feet, thrusting him across the room towards the safe. 'Now open it and don't think o' yellin' because there's nobody will hear you.'

Wordlessly, realizing that resistance was useless, Simpson took a key from his pocket and turned it in the large lock. He made to open it but Steve knocked his arm aside.

Swinging the heavy door open, Steve saw, as he had suspected, the small Derringer lying on the stack of papers.

Tossing the small weapon across the room, Steve turned sharply, reversing the Colt and bringing the butt down heavily on the other's skull. Without a sound, Simpson collapsed onto the floor at his feet.

Taking the papers over to the desk, he riffled quickly through them. Most were land deeds made out to Cal Forden and witnessed by Simpson. Without any doubt, he thought, most, if not all, of these had been obtained by fraud or coercion.

At the very bottom, however, he came across what he was looking for. He recognized his brother's handwriting immediately. Why this damning report had not been destroyed he couldn't guess unless Forden or Simpson intended to use it against Casson. Thrusting it and the deeds into his pocket, he made his way back through the kitchen to where Jefferson stood waiting impatiently outside.

'Did yuh find what yuh was lookin' for?' queried the other.

'I got everythin' I need,' Steve replied grimly. 'Enough evidence for the army to clean up this entire territory.'

CHAPTER IX

DECOY

They were halfway to where the horses were tethered when there was a sudden commotion behind them. Several men were shouting and the sounds came from near the sheriff's office.

'They've found Jessop and know you've got away,' Jefferson said in an urgent tone. He gripped Steve by the arm and pulled him forward.

Together, they ran for the horses. The shouting behind them had been taken up by others and Steve guessed that most of the town was now out on the streets.

The horses were still where they had left them. Swinging into the saddle, Steve hauled hard on the reins, putting the stallion to the upgrade with Jefferson following close behind.

He knew they would make the quickest time heading for the main trail and following it until they caught up with the wagons. But that would be what those men in Calder Wells would be expecting them to do. Furthermore, there was the distinct possibility he would lead these killers to the wagon train and, knowing these gunhawks, they wouldn't hesitate to attack it for whatever valuables those folk carried with them.

Once they came out of the trees, he gestured with his left hand, indicating they were to swing north. His companion followed him without question. At their backs, the shouting had died away but he guessed that, within a short while, there would be men on their trail, men intent on gunning them down.

He knew he should feel some sense of satisfaction at the knowledge that his brother had been avenged but crucially, there was nothing. He had given no thought to his own life and had it not been for the loyalty of the man now riding with him, he would still be in that helltown, waiting to be hanged.

Ten minutes of hard riding brought them into a region of massive boulders and looming overhangs. Here, it was only just possible for them to squeeze through narrow openings that twisted and turned like a maze, slowing them down to little more than a walk.

The faint moonlight showed little detail.

'Look yonder, Mistuh Calladine.' Jefferson twisted in his saddle and was pointing behind them.

Whirling, Steve threw a quick glance over his shoulder. Even in the dimness, the cloud of dust showed quite clearly. The riders were in a tightly knit bunch and were spurring their mounts at a cruel, punishing pace. Even that glance was sufficient to tell him there were at least half a dozen men on their trail.

A second sweeping glance showed something more. Off to the right, there was a second group of men.

'They're tryin' to cut us off,' he called sharply. 'Do you know anythin' of this place? Anywhere we can hole up?'

A pause, then, 'Follow me, quickly!' Jefferson raked spurs to his mount's flanks, forcing it towards a steep downgrade.

Without thinking, Steve followed. Ahead of them lay only the sheer outlines of the enclosing hills, climbing high towards the starlit heavens. But he had trusted this man before and now there was nothing else for him to do.

A few moments later, they entered a deep defile. Littered with boulders and upthrusting spurs of rock, it stretched away in front of them. Steve drew his lips tightly together. Now they had one bunch of pursuers at their backs and if they followed this canyon to its end, they would certainly ride straight into that second group.

Then, without warning, his companion halted, tugging hard on the reins and swinging his mount sharply to the left. A moment later, he vanished from sight, seeming to melt into the wall of solid stone.

Hauling back on the reins, Steve pulled the stallion to a rearing halt and glanced quickly to his left. There was a narrow opening, visible only as a thin slice of black shadow.

Cautiously, he worked his way along it. Jefferson

was somewhere in front of him, invisible in the pitch blackness. Then the other's voice reached him from some distance away.

'Jest keep movin'. This is the track to one o' the old gold workings. Nobody's been here in more'n twenty years.'

Gingerly, Steve pushed the stallion onward. The animal was nervous and he had to maintain a tight controlling grip on the reins. He could see nothing. Putting out a hand he felt the rough rock less than a foot away.

Gradually, however, his eyes became accustomed to the intense darkness. His companion was a dim figure a few yards in front of him. The incredibly narrow trail continued up into the hills, twisting and turning so many times that he lost all conception of direction.

It would have to end somewhere, he thought, and then, if any of those gunmen on their trail knew anything of it, they would surely be trapped with no avenue of escape.

For a further five minutes, they rode on in silence. Then, abruptly, the trail ended on a wide rocky shelf. At the far end stood a large wooden shack with two smaller buildings on one side.

'What is this place?' he asked, his voice echoing hollowly from the stone overhangs.

Jefferson jerked his head around. 'There were three mine workings here in the old days. I've heard some o' the prospectors talkin' about them when I was first brought to Calder Wells. This is one of 'em.'

Steve shook his head. Now, he was confident that

his companion had unwittingly led them into a trap. 'It would be sheer suicide to hole up in that shack. If they know of this place, this is where they'd expect us to head for. Maybe we could hold 'em off for a little while but—'

'No, sir, Mistuh Calladine. That ain't what I'm thinkin'. This is just a decoy to keep 'em occupied for a while and give us a chance to get away. There's an old Indian trail yonder. We take that through the hills. My guess is they'll head straight for here as soon as those two groups meet up and realize we've slipped through their fingers. But while they're busy shootin' up this place, thinkin' we're inside and ready for 'em, we'll have a good head start.'

'Then we'd better—' Steve broke off sharply. A sound reached them from somewhere back along the trail. It was faint and distorted by echoes but it brought him instantly upright in the saddle.

'Reckon they have met up and found nothin',' Jefferson murmured in a low voice.

'And they'll either think we've slipped through their trap or we're up here.'

Out on the trail, Jessop peered angrily into the darkness. His head still thumped incessantly like a hammer on an anvil where he had been slugged in his office. When Danvers and Skelton had gone after Collins that morning, he had anticipated no problems, had expected them to finish the other off without any trouble.

It had been a simple enough job, riding after an unarmed man and there had been nowhere in the

Badlands where Collins could hide. Yet they hadn't returned and this Jefferson Collins had walked boldly into his office brandishing a Colt, demanding he should release his prisoner.

When he had refused, the other had slugged him on the side of the head with a gunbutt, taken the keys, and let the stranger go.

Now Forden was on his back for allowing this prisoner to escape. Where Collins had met up with this stranger who had shot Lobo, he didn't know. The only conclusion he could reach was that this gunslinger had somehow jumped Skelton and Danvers, killing them both.

He ground his teeth in a surge of anger. He'd felt certain that once he had decided those two men would not make for the main trail and by splitting his force, he could trap them along this ravine.

Staring across at the men in the other group, he rasped, 'You're sure they didn't give you the slip back yonder?'

'Not a chance,' replied one of the men.

Gripping the reins tightly as his mount jerked nervously, Jessop strained his ears to pick out any sound of drumming hoofs in the distance that might tell him the two men had broken cover and were spurring away. But there was nothing apart from their own harsh breathing and the blowing of the horses.

'Then they're still around here someplace, probably holed up in the rocks. They must have slipped off this trail somewhere. Spread out on both sides and—'

'Sheriff,' one of the men butted in. 'It could be

they've taken the trail up to the old mine workings.'

Swiftly, Jessop rode forward. 'Then if they have, we've got 'em. They've sealed their own death warrants because there ain't no way out o' there that I know of.'

He gestured to the men to follow him, heading for the track into the hills, pausing every so often to scan the ground for any sign that someone had ridden that way recently.

'You reckon they'd be fool enough to go into the old workings?' asked one of the men dubiously.

'If they went this way, it's the only place they can have gone,' said the sheriff savagely. 'Any o' you men know this place?'

When there was no answer, he drew in a deep breath. 'This ain't going to be easy.' He spoke to no one in particular. 'We'll have to flush 'em out. No doubt they'll be waitin' for us at the end of this track and they could pick us off the minute we show our faces.'

'Mebbe it would be better if we were to—'

'Goddamnit! There are twelve of us against two o' them and it would surprise me if that Collins has ever fired a gun in his life. Now let's get movin', or we'll all answer to Forden in the mornin'.'

Putting their mounts to the upgrade, they rode at a steady pace, eyes watching the rocks on either side in the event of an ambush. At the end of the track, they dismounted and moved forward cautiously, guns ready in their hands.

Crouching down, Jessop eyed the shadowed shack speculatively. There was no sign of life about it. The rest of the men slid into the rocks on either side of him, keeping their heads down.

'Don't see any sign o' their mounts,' observed the man on Jessop's left.

'Damnation, Clint, you don't expect them to leave their horses in full sight, do you?' Jessop snapped coldly.

Keeping his head well down, he called loudly, 'We know you're in there, Calladine, you and Collins. Either come out with your hands raised or we'll blast you both to hell.'

He expected a shot to greet his ultimatum but there was nothing. Wriggling a little to one side, he said, 'All of you men get ready to rush that shack when I give the word. First, we'll show 'em we mean business. Put a few shots into the place and those other buildings.'

The ensuing roar of gunfire almost deafened him, the hammering echoes slamming back and forh between the surrounding hills. Wood splintered and chips flew in all directions. What remained of the glass in the windows shattered into fragments.

When the fusillade ended and there had been no return fire, Jessop felt a twinge of doubt enter his mind. His head was ringing from the din and it had not made the agony in his skull from the blow he'd received earlier any better.

'Could be there ain't anybody there,' remarked one of the posse.

'Or it could mean they don't intend to waste any ammunition on targets they can't see,' Jessop answered. 'There's only one way to find out.'

He noticed the men glancing uncertainly at each other. Clearly, they were all thinking that if those two men were trapped inside that building behind those stout wooden walls, it would be a massacre if they tried a frontal attack.

He waved an arm impatiently. 'Me and Jed will give you coverin' fire. Now move!'

Reluctantly, the men got their feet under them, waited tensely for several moments, then lunged forward, heads low, racing for the shack.

Jessop loosed off a couple of shots, aiming at the windows. He saw the first two men reach the door and throw themselves down, huddling against the wall. Then one got to his feet and kicked savagely at the door. It swung open at once and the men burst in.

Five minutes later, they emerged, shaking their heads, expressions of bewilderment on their features.

'This danged place is empty, Sheriff,' one shouted harshly. 'Nobody has been in here for years.'

'Then where the hell?' Jessop pushed himself to his feet, swayed a little as a wave of agony lanced through the side of his head. Straightening with an effort, he stormed towards the shack.

Once inside, he struck a match and held it out in front of him. By its feeble light, he was able to satisfy himself that the man was right. Dust lay everywhere. Over against the wall were a couple of rusty iron beds with tattered blankets thrown over them.

There was a second smaller room at the rear but apart from rusted mining equipment, it was also empty.

After sending two men to check the outbuildings, he stormed, 'Then where are they? This is the only way they could've come.'

'Well, they ain't here, Sheriff,' muttered one of the men, holstering his Colts. 'From the looks o' this place, they never came this far.'

'Goddamnit! There's no way we could've missed them along the trail.' He walked back to the horses. 'Ain't no sense stayin' here,' he called over his shoulder. 'Tomorrow we get ourselves an Indian scout who can pick up their trail.'

'Why go to all that trouble, Sheriff?' Jed muttered. 'We'll never catch up with 'em now. They'll be clear out o' the territory.'

Jessop swung on him viciously. 'Because unless I miss my guess, that's what Cal Forden will want. He's just lost his best man and he ain't going to forget that and let it go.' A crafty glint came into his eyes as a fresh thought occurred to him. 'I also reckon someone should get word to Seth Yarrow, his brother. Could be he'll want to even things up with this *hombre* just as much as Forden.'

CHAPTER X

INDIAN TRAIL

Cal Forden rode into Calder Wells almost an hour after Jessop and the posse had ridden out. The news that his best man had been shot down in the saloon and was now lying in the mortuary had put him in a foul temper. Puffing furiously on his cigar, he now sat in the sheriff's seat, scarcely able to contain his fury and impatience.

This was something he had never anticipated. No one had ever faced up to Lobo before and walked away. Either this man had shot the other down without giving him any warning as most of his men claimed, or Calladine was even faster with a gun than Lobo was with a knife. Either way, this stranger had to be eliminated before he could cause any more trouble.

Outside, the street was deathly quiet. After a time, the silence began to eat at his frayed nerves. Lighting the cigar where it had gone out, he glared at the man standing near the office door.

'You say this stranger claimed to be that Federal marshal's brother, Flint?'

'That's what he said, boss. Somehow, he knew it was Lobo who knifed that lawman and he also knew that Lobo never carried a gun.'

Forden pondered that for a moment, his flushed features frozen in a mask of deep concentration. Finally, speaking around the cigar, he muttered, 'Then it's possible he came here simply for revenge. Maybe he ain't no marshal like the other one.'

He made to say something more, then jerked up his head at the sound of approaching riders. There was the sound of footsteps outside on the boardwalk and a moment later the door opened and Jessop came in.

'Well?' Forden snarled. 'Did you get him?'

Jessop shook his head nervously. 'We trailed 'em up into the old gold mine at Fender's Bluff but they gave us the slip. We figgered they was inside the shack but they must've ridden on and taken one o' the old Indians trails across the hills.'

Forden's face flushed an even deeper shade of purple. With a savage movement, he stubbed out his cigar. 'You had him locked in one of the cells, then you let him escape and now you tell me he's given you the slip. What kind o' fools am I surrounded with? I gave you this job to keep trouble out o' Calder Wells.'

Jessop fiddled with his hat before tossing it onto the desk. 'How was I to know he had someone with him. I figured he'd ridden into town alone.'

Forden leaned forward across the desk, his eyes boring into the sheriff. 'You say there were two of 'em?'

'That's right. He's with that swamper who rode out of town yesterday mornin'. I sent a couple o' men after Collins but they must've run into this *hombre* before they had a chance to kill him. He bust into the office and hit me on the head before lettin' Calladine out o' the cell.'

'Goddamnit! Do I have to do everythin' in this town myself?' For a moment, Forden seemed on the point of striking the sheriff. Then he managed to control himself. 'All right. Rest up your mounts and then be ready to move out at first light. I want these two hunted down and brought back, dead or alive. You got that, Jessop?'

Jessop gave a brief nod of acquiescence.

'Good. Take Sam Otuchi with you. If anyone can follow a trail, he can. Maybe there's no real harm done but I want that killer brought in and hanged. It may be that—'

There was a sudden commotion outside. The door swung open and Simpson staggered in, helped by two of the men. There was a streak of blood down one side of his face and he seemed barely conscious.

'What the hell?' Forden began.

'Slim found him like this,' said one of the men. 'It looked as if his safe had been ransacked.'

Forden's breath hissed through his teeth. For a moment, his gaze locked with Jessop's and he knew the same thought had occurred to the sheriff. To one of the watching men, he snapped, 'Get a bucket of water and throw it over him. I want to know exactly what happened and what was stolen from that safe.'

Ten minutes of hard questioning and Forden knew the worst. Setting his teeth into a wolfish grimace, he sat rigid in the chair, his mind a riot of thoughts and conjectures. With those deeds and, in particular, that damning marshal's report in the wrong hands, he could see his whole empire crumbling into dust before his eyes.

He reached a sudden decision. Getting swiftly to his feet, he snapped an order to the man standing next to the door. 'Ride back to the ranch, Flint,' he ordered tersely. 'Round up all the men you can and ride out around the north of the hills and then cut south. If you ride fast you should cut off these two before they reach the trail. They can't ride quickly through the hills.

'The rest of you come with me. There's no time to rest the horses now. You too, Jessop. We'll take Sam Otuchi with us and follow their trail through the mine workings. Between us, we should run them down.'

Grinning viciously, he added, 'There'll be a bonus for the man who kills Calladine and Collins.'

Dawn crept in greyly from the east. An hour earlier, the stars had disappeared and the sky had turned overcast. A cold rain now seeped down upon the hills and even the brightening daylight only served to make distant details indistinct.

Throughout the night, there had been no indication of pursuit but Steve was certain they were still not out of danger. Those papers in his pocket were pure dynamite where Casson and Forden were concerned. Neither man would spare any effort to prevent them falling into the hands of the army or the Federal authorities.

The trail they were following was scarcely discernible. At times there was no sign of it yet Jefferson still seemed confident as he led the way, angling between tall, spearing columns of granite, pushing through narrow, steep-sided ravines that slashed the ground in all directions.

Half an hour later, they reined their mounts where a massive slab of rock stood, balanced seemingly precariously over a shelving layer of granite. Here they dismounted and led their horses out of the drizzling rain into shelter. Squatting with his back against the rock, Jefferson said solemnly, 'I reckon we've thrown Jessop and his men off our trail but there could be others.'

Chewing on the jerked beef from his saddlebag, Steve nodded. 'Forden will know everythin' by now. He'll be mad enough about Lobo's death but once that lawyer comes round, he'll be not only angry, but also scared.'

'And frightened men who see their cattle empire slippin' away from 'em, will do anythin' to prevent it,' Collins answered.

Swallowing the food down with water, Steve said, 'You seem to know this country pretty well. If you were in Forden's shoes, what would you do?'

The other deliberated the question for a while, then shrugged. 'I guess I'd split my force. It's a good thirty mile ride around these hills to the north but I don't think that would put him off.'

'And the second bunch?'

Collins grinned, showing his white teeth. 'There's an old Indian trapper in town. Sam Otuchi. If anyone can track us through these hills, he's the man to do it. He could lead Jessop and his posse to us without any trouble.'

Steve turned that over in his mind. Everything the other said made sense. Forden was no fool. Acting in this way, he could trap them in these hills and it would be only a matter of time before they were flushed out.

Tightening his lips, he asked, 'How far do these hills extend to the west?'

'Another couple o' miles. Then yuh hit the Badlands and if yuh figger on losin' them in there, yuh'd better think again. There's no cover there.'

'So we leave this trail here and cut either north or south.'

Collins' broad features twisted into a scowl of concentration. 'That's real rough country to the north and if Forden does send his men that way, we could run smack into 'em.'

Steve had already considered that possibility. 'But that's the way he won't be expectin' us to go. With luck, he'll figure we'll stick with this trail to its end and then break out into the open country.'

'Ain't you forgettin' Sam Otuchi? Maybe you could fool Jessop but not him. He'll pick up our tracks as easily as if they're marked out in the rocks.'

Steve got stiffly to his feet. 'Reckon that's a chance

we'll have to take. Let's get movin'.'

One glance at the crowding rocks that bordered the trail was sufficient to tell them they would have to walk their mounts. If the rough track from the old mine workings had been bad, the going here was a thousand times more difficult. With no trail to follow, it was a case of edging their mounts through narrow apertures and over razor-edged boulders.

Their sodden clothing clung about their bodies, hampering every movement. With the rain came the wind, savage gusts that tore at them from every direction. Fortunately, both animals were sure-footed brutes, picking a way forward where none seemed to exist.

Several times they had to halt and scan the terrain ahead of them, searching for some route that would lead them through the maze of ragged stone columns and funnelling crevices. By the time an hour had passed, both men were so weary they could hardly stand. The horses, too, were finding it difficult to go on.

They were still high up in the hills but to their left the ground dropped away precipitously. Less than two miles away in that direction was the beginning of the Badlands. Flat and featureless, they stretched clear to the western horizon; a region of brown scrub and arid, waterless soil, bleached almost white by the long days of pitiless sun and heat.

Five minutes later, they came upon a small plateau, shielded on all sides by high ridges. Here, they halted. Dropping down onto his knees, Jefferson said hoarsely, 'Could be we made a mistake comin' this way, Mistuh Calladine. There ain't no way through these hills.'

Steve took a swig from the canteen. Wiping his mouth on the back of his hand, he made to say something, then lowered his head quickly. 'Riders!' he said throatily. 'And movin' fast.'

Very cautiously, Jefferson lifted himself, leaning against the granite ledge, raising his head slowly until his chin was resting on the top. Screwing up his eyes against the beating rain, he murmured, 'That's Forden leading 'em. Reckon we were right. They're hopin' to cut us off at the end o' that trail.'

Steve studied the riders closely. He estimated there were at least thirty men with Forden. The rancher must have pulled most of his men together and ridden out immediately he had learned that those important papers were missing.

Clenching his teeth, Steve said thinly, 'It won't be long before they meet up with the others and with that Indian trackin' us, they'll be on top of us within an hour.'

Jefferson turned his head slowly, surveying their surroundings. 'Reckon the only thing we can do is stash the horses out o' sight and wait. We have a better chance makin' a stand here than if we're attacked from behind.'

Steve knew it would be merely a futile gesture. Once their ammunition was spent, they would be finished. But what was the alternative? They would undoubtedly be overtaken long before they got out of this treacherous region and on the Badlands, in full view of their pursuers, they would stand no chance at all.

Ten minutes later, they had the horses out of sight among the rocks. Then they settled down to wait, crouching behind the cover of the high ledge on the end of the plateau. Interminably slowly, the minutes lengthened into an hour. The rain eased and then ceased altogether.

Gradually, the utter silence began to eat at Steve's nerves, already stretched to breaking point. By now, Forden would have linked up with Jessop and the posse riding in from the other direction. Once Sam Otuchi came upon the spot where they had pulled off the trail, those men would be edging towards them.

Beside him, Jefferson lay flat on his stomach behind the ledge. He held both heavy Colts in his hands, his forefingers through the trigger guards. How well he would use them when the time came, Steve didn't know. He checked his own, then jerked up his head swiftly. A faint sound had reached him from further down the hillside.

'Did yuh hear somethin', Mistuh Calladine?' Jefferson whispered.

'I thought I picked out the sound of a horse yonder,' Steve replied, equally softly.

'Couldn't be sure, but—'

The sound was not repeated but he was still unable to relax. There had been something and. . . .

He stiffened abruptly as a voice from behind them said softly, 'Keep those guns where they are, both o' you.'

Slowly, Steve turned his head, the rest of his body

145

rigid. The short figure stood on top of a high rock less than five yards away. There was a rifle trained on them and the hands that held it were rock steady. Although they had never met, Steve knew immediately who the other was. Sam Otuchi! And that meant there were other men all around them.

In an avalanche of small rocks, the Indian slithered down the side of the rock, landing lightly on his feet beside them. There was a faint grin on his leathery features. Tensely, knowing there was nothing they could do, Steve waited for the rest of Forden's men to put in an appearance.

'You can put your guns away,' the other said, lowering the rifle. 'There is no one with me. I sent them all on a false trail. By now they'll be miles away to the south.'

'You sent them on a false trail.' Steve repeated the other's words stupidly, scarcely able to believe his ears. 'But why? I don't understand.'

Before replying, Otuchi lifted his free hand and touched the long cruel scar down one cheek. Then he drew his leather jerkin aside and indicated a second one along his left side. 'Lobo did this. He thought it good sport to mark my people with his knife. The Apache do not forget when someone like you kills their enemy.'

Letting his breath gush out in a long exhalation, Steve brushed the rain from his eyes.

'You knew we'd turned off the trail back there.'

'I knew. But I say nothing to the sheriff and those other men. Jessop and Forden both have evil spirits in them. I say I ride back into town but I came to find

146

you. Now you follow me.'

The Indian moved back into the rocks for his mount. Turning to Jefferson, Steve asked softly, 'Do you think we can trust this Indian?'

'We got no other choice, Mistuh Calladine. But if anyone has cause to hate Lobo, it's him.'

Fetching their horses, they waited. A moment later, Sam Otuchi came back, leading a palomino. Progress was slow as they followed the Indian through some of the most rugged and treacherous terrain Steve had ever known. Yet somehow, they reached the bottom without mishap.

Here a narrow stream gushed down the hillside and their guide indicated they were to drink their fill and top up their canteens with the cold, clear water. 'Now we must cross part of the Badlands,' he told them. 'It will be two days before we find any water.'

'It shouldn't be too bad in this rain,' Steve observed as they mounted up.

Sam Otuchi shook his head. 'Rain will soon stop,' he affirmed confidently.

Putting spurs to their mounts, Steve and Jefferson followed the Indian into the wide wilderness of the Badlands.

CHAPTER XI

SAND AND SUNBLAZE

Sam Otuchi had spoken the truth about the rain. Half an hour later, it cleared away eastward over the rugged hills and the sun came out in a pale blue sky. Very soon, it beat down onto their backs and heads with a fiery touch. All around them, the wilderness began to glare in the brilliance.

Fine grey dust rose under the feet of their mounts, building into a cloud that hung about them as they progressed deeper into the Badlands. It got into their mouths and nostrils, clogged their throats, worked its way into their eyes until they were red and burning.

What little moisture had penetrated the ground during the rain soon evaporated until the earth was as dry as a bleached bone. Now time seemed to melt and flow into a continuous wave of heat.

Soon, Steve was riding low in the saddle, bent

forward over the stallion's neck to minimize the sunglare. Behind them, the range of hills receded into the distance until it was no more than a vague, shimmering blur.

A little way in front of him, Sam Otuchi rode tall on his mount, his broad figure seemingly immune to the conditions. His hawklike face was set towards the west, utterly expressionless, only his dark eyes moving as he swept the area with a keen, penetrating gaze, alert for trouble. Occasionally, he would throw a quick glance to their left. Each time, he would give a slight nod, evidently satisfied there was no sign of Forden and his crew.

Hour after hour, their guide led them on, allowing no stops. Inwardly, Steve wondered where Forden and his men were now. Sooner or later, they would realize they had been sent on a wild goose chase and it wouldn't be long before the rancher realized they had been fooled by Sam Otuchi. Steve guessed he would then either retrace his steps or figure out they had fled into the Badlands.

That thought brought a fresh wave of apprehension into his mind. Here in this flat wilderness, the three of them would be sitting targets. The only advantage he and his companions had was that their mounts were comparatively fresh compared with those men looking for them. Whether it would give them sufficient edge to get away was something only time would tell.

By mid-afternoon, they had covered the best part of ten miles but with the sun still close to its zenith, the heat had become intolerable. Sweat dripped continuously into their eyes and their shirts were clinging uncomfortably to their bodies. Then, holding up his right hand, Sam Otuchi called a halt.

'We rest here for a little while,' he said in a flat monotone. 'There is still no sign those others are headed this way.'

Wearily, Steve slid to the ground, flexing the muscles of his legs where hard fingers of cramp were biting into them. Mopping his face, he lowered himself to the dust. 'How long do you figure before they discover they're on the wrong trail?' he asked hoarsely through dust-caked lips.

'If they follow that trail it will lead them back to Calder Wells. That is when they will know for certain. Neither of you would return there, it would be much too dangerous for you.'

'Then they will come,' Jefferson spoke thickly.

'Perhaps.' The Indian's tone was not as certain as Jefferson's. 'You forget they have been riding fast all night. I think they will need fresh horses before they can follow us into this wilderness.'

Steve immediately saw the logic behind the other's words. Forden was now a man with a mission. Whatever happened, he had to get his hands on the documents that could seal his fate. He would recognize the danger of setting out into the Badlands after them on mounts that could drop beneath him and his men long before they reached the other side.

A man would be a fool to venture into this barren, arid wilderness on bone-weary horses. They would never make it and could find themselves in serious trouble if they attempted it. But there was nothing as sure that he would waste no time pursuing them.

Squatting on the heat-baked ground, they ate a little of their remaining food, drinking sparingly from their canteens. Steve's mouth was so parched the water seemed to be wholly absorbed before it reached his throat.

Ten minutes later, they were in the saddle again, pushing their weary mounts to the limit. The horses were finding the going difficult, the gritty dust working its way into their hoofs. Here and there were clumps of spiny cactus while chamise and mesquite dotted the areas between green-yellow cacti.

Towards evening, a slight coolness entered the superheated air but with it came a gusting wind that hurled the gritty earth into their faces. There was no protection against it as the irritating grains worked their way into every fold in their flesh.

Night fell swiftly once the sun had set amid a blaze of red and yellow. The stars came out in their thousands and the temperature dropped sharply. Soon, Steve and Jefferson were shivering violently as the sweat congealed on their limbs.

Sam Otuchi continued for almost an hour before signaling a halt. Stretching his aching legs, Steve peered into the darkness. A little way ahead there appeared to be a wide shadow lying over the ground. Several moments passed before he realized it was a deep depression angling away to their right.

Keeping a tight hold on the reins, they led the horses into it. Sam Otuchi, a dim figure in the pale starlight, walked up to Steve where he stood beside Jefferson. 'You must sleep now,' he said tonelessly.

'Tomorrow will be just as bad as today. I will keep watch for any danger.'

Taking his blanket from the saddlebag, Steve rolled himself into it, lying on his back and staring up at the stars. So much had happened since that dismal day when he had joined that wagon train in Clinton. He had done what he had set out to do. By killing Lobo he had avenged his brother's death but in doing so he had landed himself into far deeper trouble than he had anticipated.

Not only had he been branded a cold-blooded killer with a price on his head but there was Cal Forden determined to kill him before he could get the papers to the proper authorities. And somewhere in the background was Seth Yarrow, Lobo's brother, just as determined to kill him as he had been to kill his brother's murderer.

It was with these thoughts running through his mind that he fell asleep. When he woke it was still dark but, pushing himself up onto his elbows, he made out a faint flush along the horizon. In this hour before dawn, the temperature was bearable. Getting to his feet, he built himself a cigarette, drawing the smoke deeply into his lungs.

Jefferson was already awake, moving restlessly around. A few yards away, Sam Otuchi sat on a broad slab of stone, his dimly-visible features as inscrutable as ever.

Steve doubted if he had moved an inch during the night. He was like a statue hewn from stone.

Finally, he stirred himself, drawing his jerkin more tightly about his body. 'We must leave soon,' he said softly. 'Those killers will not wait for ever.'

Finishing what little food remained, they were soon in the saddle, still heading west. Stillness, deep and tangible, closed in about them. In every direction, nothing moved in the rapidly brightening daylight.

Shortly after sunrise, the heat head began to build up once more. Now the horses moved more slowly. They had had no water for twenty-four hours and it was beginning to tell. Furthermore, they now encountered large clumps of tall, prickly cactus, higher than themselves, the ground between them interspersed with chamise and mesquite.

Conversation was now almost non-existent. Sam Otuchi led the way, his face set in grim lines. Side by side, Steve and Jefferson followed his uncompromising back.

By the end of the morning, the heat had sucked all of the moisture from their bodies. The urge to gulp down all of the water remaining in his canteen was almost more than Steve could bear. With a supreme effort, he lifted his head and peered through red-rimmed eyes into the sunglare.

There was a faint smudge on the skyline almost directly ahead, but in the shimmering heat waves it was impossible to make out anything definite. In his bemused mind, Steve had the feeling it was nothing more than a mirage that could fade at any moment. But it remained and grew larger as they progressed. Soon, he was able to discern what it was. A range of hills, their lower slopes thickly dotted with trees, their tops grey and bare of vegetation.

Now their backward glances became more frequent. Each time they expected to see a dark smudge on the otherwise empty wilderness that would indicate the position of a large group of riders spurring after them. But the minutes passed and still there was nothing.

It was beginning to look as if they were going to make it after all, that all of the heat and discomfort had been worthwhile. Time passed slowly, but eventually the tree-covered slopes were clearly visible less than a mile away.

Steve twisted in the saddle and threw a swift look at Jefferson, saw the glint of teeth as the other gave a broad grin. 'Not much further now, Mistuh Calladine,' he called. 'Reckon we're goin' to make it.'

'Do not be too certain.' The Indian spoke without turning his head. He lifted an arm and pointed.

Steve turned his head quickly to follow the direction of the other's pointing finger. For several moments, he could see nothing. Then, far off close to the horizon, he made out the small, moving blur. The riders were almost at the limit of his vision but there was no mistaking them.

'Do you reckon they've spotted us?' Jefferson asked in a low voice.

The Indian studied the distant group of riders for several moments before replying. 'It would seem they are heading towards the southern edge of this range. I would think we are too close to it for them to make us out against the background. They will not reach the hills before nightfall no matter how hard they push their mounts.'

Steve let his breath go through tightly clenched teeth. Moving slowly so as not to give themselves away, they entered the welcome safety of the tall pines.

It was late the next morning when they hit the broad track leading west. Bending low over the pony's neck, Sam Otuchi studied the ground, then gave a satisfied nod. 'Many wagons have passed this way,' he said soberly. 'Not many hours ago.'

'Then that train can't be far away.' Steve lifted his head to peer into the distance. Here, the region was a maze of tall buttes of red sandstone and there, barely a couple of miles away, he detected the cloud of dust hanging in the still air.

As they rode swiftly towards it, Steve tried to quell the rising apprehension in his mind. He knew he was almost certainly leading Forden and his hired killers to the train and there now seemed little chance that Ridgeway had got through to Fort Augusta. If he had succeeded the soldiers should now be riding with the train but he saw no sign of them as he rode up.

Detaching himself from the front of the train, Disforth rode up. 'Glad you made it back, Calladine,' he called loudly. 'Did you find that snake who killed your brother?'

'I found him,' Steve replied grimly, 'with the help o' my friend here. But there's a bunch o' gunslingers on our tail. I got the evidence I need against Casson and Forden but they don't aim to let it fall into the wrong hands. You could be in trouble if they find me here.'

'It looks like they've already found us.' Disforth pointed back along the trail.

The riders were still distant but there was no doubting their intentions. Turning in the saddle, Disforth issued a string of sharp orders. Within five minutes, the wagons were strung out in a line across the trail, all of the men were down beneath the wheels, rifles and Colts in their hands, and the women and children were under canvas.

Steve stared in amazement, a lump in his throat. This was something he had not anticipated, all of these folk willing to risk their lives and fight for him. Swiftly, he dismounted and ran for the nearest wagon. Jefferson and Sam Otuchi dropped down beside him a second later.

As the riders drew nearer, Steve made out Sheriff Jessop riding alongside a hard-faced man he guessed was Cal Forden. The latter held up his right hand while they were still a hundred yards away.

Forden pushed his mount forward a little way, then called, 'We want no trouble with anyone travellin' in those wagons. All we're after is one man, a killer wanted for murder back in Calder Wells. Turn him over to us and the rest of you can go.'

'Reckon we ain't goin' to do that, mister.' Disforth's voice rang out, loud and clear. 'We know when a man is a killer and when he's been framed.'

Forden hesitated at that, then went on, 'Don't be a fool. Calladine ain't worth you all riskin' your lives. If we don't get him within the next ten seconds, we'll blast you all the hell.'

'Try it and you'll get more than you bargained for,'

Disforth yelled. 'We've fought off the Cherokee, reckon you ain't much better.'

Forden sat absolutely still for several seconds. Then he shouted an order to the men with him. Even as they turned their mounts, pulling their Colts from their holsters, a withering volley of fire came from the wagons.

Almost a dozen men tumbled from the saddle as the lead tore into them. Lying flat beside Jefferson, Steve swung his Colt swiftly in a short arc, loosing off half a dozen shots in rapid succession. He saw Jessop suddenly rear up, his head going back as his body arched. His Colt hit the ground a split second before he did.

Two other men toppled sideways, their feet caught in the stirrups as their frightened mounts wheeled away, dragging their bodies through the dust. Forden was still yelling, motioning his men down, recognizing that while in the saddle they presented excellent targets.

Swiftly, the remaining men spread out, dropping to the ground. Now their return fire poured into the wagon train. Crouched behind the wheel, Steve saw a head lift as the man tried to find a target. Gently, he squeezed the trigger, saw the head go back. Beside him, both Jefferson and Sam Otuchi were firing rapidly as slugs hummed dangerously close to their heads.

It was soon abundantly clear, however, that despite their early losses, Forden's men still outnumbered them by five to one. They had no chance of fighting off this bunch. Very soon, Forden would give the order for his men to rush the wagon train and when that happened, they were finished.

Almost as if the rancher had divined his thought, Steve saw Forden give a signal with his left hand. Backed by a savage volley of covering fire, a score of men suddenly thrust themselves to their feet.

Ramming fresh shells into his Colts, Steve wiped the sweat from his eyes, thinning his lips as he waited. He saw the men spread out into a wide line, crouching down as they prepared to storm forward.

The crashing din of rifle fire suddenly increased tremendously in volume. Wincing, he lifted the Colts, then stared in amazement as the running men seemed to halt in their tracks, lurching drunkenly. Somewhere in the distance, a bugle sounded and then there seemed to be mounted soldiers everywhere.

Minutes later, it was all over. Forden and his men had been rounded up, surrounded by a ring of troopers. Their weapons lay in the dirt at their feet.

Going forward, Steve waited as Ridgeway rode up with a cavalry major beside him. The officer dismounted. At his side, Ridgeway said, 'This is Major Weston. I told him you were hopin' to get your hands on evidence to convict Forden and Casson of runnin' guns to the Indians and obtaining land by fraud.'

'Is that correct, Mister Calladine?' Weston asked.

Nodding, Steve took the documents and his brother's report from his pocket and handed them over. The other glanced rapidly through them, pursing his lips. Finally, he folded them carefully and placed them inside his tunic.

'You did well,' he said. 'You won't be having any more trouble from them, I can guarantee that. As for that false murder charge against you, I'll see that's quashed.'

'Thanks.' Steve gave a brief nod. 'I'm only glad my brother didn't die for nothin'.'

Touching his hat in a brief salute, the major turned back to his men and a few minutes later, with Forden and his crew mounted with their hands tied, they rode off.

Steve watched them go, then turned to find Melanie standing close beside him. 'It's finished for you now,' she said softly. 'Will you be riding back east, or—'

There was a light in her eyes he had never seen before. 'I guess I'll stay with the train,' he said. 'Now that I've—' He broke off sharply as a harsh voice said, 'You ain't goin' nowhere, Calladine. This is the end o' the trail for you.'

Seth Yarrow stepped into sight a few yards away, where he had somehow managed to secrete himself during the fighting. 'Don't anybody try to go for their guns. The girl gets it first and then you.'

Steve felt a wash of futile anger sear through him as the other stepped forward a couple of paces. 'I said I'd get the rattler who shot my brother back in Calder Wells. Now I aim to keep my promise.'

The Colt in Yarrow's hand moved slightly until it was pointing directly at Melanie. Steve knew the other meant every word. Even if he managed to pull the girl behind him, it was only a matter of seconds before they were both dead. He saw the other's finger tighten on the trigger, saw the malicious smile on Yarrow's thin lips.

He flinched instinctively as the shot rang out. For a moment, he thought Melanie slumped against him, then realized she was still standing. Yarrow was clutching at his chest where blood oozed between his locked fingers. He stood there for an instant, then all of the starch went out of him as he crashed onto his face in the dirt.

Slowly, Steve turned his head, wondering where the shot had come from. Then he saw the one man Yarrow had not bothered to watch. Very slowly, the preacher tossed the smoking Colt away.

'There are times,' he said solemnly, 'when a man of God cannot be a man of peace.'

'You did right, Reverend,' Ridgeway said. He threw a swift glance behind him.

'Guess you might have another duty to perform before we get very far along the trail.'

CORK CITY LIBRARIES

®